Rita Donovan

the
Plague Saint

TESSERACT BOOKS
an imprint of
The Books Collective
Edmonton
1997

Tesseract Books and the Books Collective acknowledge the support of the
Alberta Foundation for the Arts for its grants to publishers. We
acknowledge the support of the Canada Council for the Arts for our
publishing programme.

Thanks to Screaming Colour Inc. (a division of Quality Color Press Inc.),
and Daana Downey and Kim Smith at Priority Printing.

Cover art: "One Clown: Death", 40"x80"Polaroid print,
copyright ©1990 by Evergon.
Cover and title page design: Gerry Dotto.
Editor for the press: John Park.
Inside design and page set-up by Ike at the Wooden Door, in Ogilvy (a
True-Type Font) in Word for Windows 6. Printed at Priority Printing,
Edmonton, on 50lb. Offset White with softcovers of Cornwall Cover and
hardcovers in buckram with Luna Gloss dustjackets.

Published in Canada by Tesseract Books, an imprint of the Books
Collective, 214-21, 10405 Jasper Avenue, Edmonton, Alberta,
Canada T5J 3S2. Telephone (403) 448 0590. Tesseract Books are
distributed in Canada by H.B.Fenn&Co., 34 Nixon Road, Bolton,
Ontario L7E 1W2. Ph. 1-800-267-FENN, and in the US by
Koen Book Distributors Ltd., 10 Twosome Drive, P.O.Box 600,
Mooretown, NJ 08057.

Canadian Cataloguing in Publication Data

Donovan, Rita, 1955-
 The plague saint

 ISBN 1-895836-29-8 (bound). –ISBN 1-895836-28-X (pbk.)

I. Title.
PS8557.O58P62 1997   C813'.54   C97-910611-7
PR9119.3.D5554P62 1997

Dedication:

For Dianne and for Annie
companions on the road;
and
for John

Acknowledgements:

The author would like to acknowledge grants from The Canada Council, the
Ontario Arts Council and the Regional Municipality of Ottawa Carleton which
aided in the production of this work.

The author would also like to thank John Park
for his editing and his patience.

part 1

The walls breathed and when they breathed the pestis *moved like a vine along the garden floor, like a vein in the body, and* bubo *and* carbone *blossomed in the groin, chestnuts of pain, blisters of agony, greater than the Duomo floating outside the window.* Maxima et horribilis, *the Sign upon the carder, upon the pale woolsorter, the blackened body beneath gold brocade. The* pestis *and all of the other plagues, smallpox, 'the plague of little children'.* "Pesticula, pesticula", *praying for a little plague, prostrate before the saints in the Duomo,* "per piacere". *Holy Names around the neck, the hand exploring pustule, cupping gently over* petecchiae, *holding haemorrhage,* Grazie a Dio!, *mercy ringing down from the bells.*

Or the bell. The single clink, the scurrying chatter of the bell, tied to the gravedigger edging along the Via Maria. And now the rhythm changes, is it a limp, the drop of an infected leg? Or a body, blackened, swollen, calm at last after fever, the wail of the widow as the husband is stripped of his best woven shirt, is thrown into the fields outside consecrated ground.

The dirt on his eyes. The earth has not covered his eyes.

"He is naked!" her hand to her mouth, a gesture frequent when they love. "The dogs!" she cries, and is led, herself, to the lazaretto, *the bell, the little bell like an evil-throated bird.*

*

The question was simple. Was he a Creeder? Lily couldn't tell when she looked at people. He had ordered her to stay in the motel room. Don't move, he said. She thought of his eyes, so wide, so open. That used to be a good sign, she remembered.

Lily's arm still ached from the sudden vault she had been forced to take over the retaining wall at the last place. As she paced, she swung her arm back and forth. She hated this. Something about this room, the painting of canal boats in a world not like her own, the lampshade brimming with dust-bright bugs. What was he? A member of the Church of the Survivors; a follower of Ren Bogen and his droning song of freedom? He swore he was not, maintaining his solidarity with the Underground. He had shown her the rope marks on his wrists. "They tried," he bristled. "They wanted information."

But who didn't, who didn't want information?

On the corner where the newspaper booths once stood, small kiosks jutted out. They were ubiquitous; she barely noticed them now, though when they were first built they had instilled such fear. Lists. Lists of people who had the disease. Names of those who would be sent into quarantine, of those who might eventually pass the purification tribunal. She was on a quarantine list now. She and Beatrice.

They walked an arc around a middle-aged man sitting on the curb. His possessions were spread on a blanket beside him — three shoes, an antique watch and fob, a frayed vest with all of the buttons gone.

"Please. Something, anything you've got. Something perishable? Fruit?"

Lily almost laughed at the absurdity. Fruit? Something perishable? Yes, like the man.

"I need vitamins," he quietly volunteered. "I need an amethyst. Please."

Lily's companion slogged on past the beggar.

Creeder! Lily swore silently.

As if hearing her, he turned back, shrugged his pack from his right shoulder and retrieved a couple of dried biscuits, which he placed in the man's lap.

They moved on.

Lily walked behind the surly man, this courier, street-brawler or traitor. She was wondering about his affiliations when she was wrenched, spinning, her pack pulled from her. Her bag! Her message to Beatrice!

The courier whirled in time to see the bandy-legged culprit limp away with Lily's pack-sack. In two leaps he was upon the wretched thief, dropping him to the pavement. Her bag was stuffed back into her arms with an out of breath, "Be more careful." Lily agreed. She would have to be more careful.

How did he expect to get her past the checkpoints? Where was he taking her?

"Christ," the man swore under his breath.

"What?"

"I was going to go this way."

The street had been cordoned off. Lily could see a crudely whitewashed cross on the door of a house partway down the street. The Sanitation Commission truck was outside, its little strobe flashing, glinting off an abandoned tricycle. The immaculate white suits and flowing capes of the workers were impressive. They carried the snow-white litter to the back of the truck, cranked open the door and slid it in. Their faces, though masked, seemed properly solemn. Lily shivered in the sudden absolute silence.

"Another one," she murmured.

"We're late," the companion motioned. Lily nodded, looking back at a small child on the steps.

How long had she been travelling? It felt like forever. Could it only have been these past few weeks, *weeks*, since she had seen Beatrice? Lily had been stuffed into hampers, into the backs of trucks, and driven through checkpoints until she had lost all sense of direction. Nobody travelled much since the epidemic. Travel meant employment, papers, medicals. The Underground, it seemed, relied on luck as much as anything.

Lily kept track of time with the memos in her VoxBox. She knew that when she next bled with the moon it would be a month since she had seen her daughter.

*

The air near the mountains was different. Thinner, somebody might have told her. Clearer and cleaner. Nobody had prepared her for how cold it was.

When all of this first started Lily had been tempted to say that she had been through it before. Things always seemed easier when you could tag on the words: like last time. But, scanning the ice-crenellated ceiling of the cave, she knew that, no, she had never been in this much trouble before.

It was useless to speculate. That was the other funny thing. Either the future was all possibility or it was not. If she had felt like laughing she would have laughed to consider that the lousy stuff she had been through might colour and even determine the ordeals that awaited. It was like being forced, as her parents had been, to relive their disco shame in all sorts of bad business and personal decisions.

She remembered, it was one of her first memories actually, the sight of her parents heading out the door, Mona in a rust-coloured lamé dress, Jack in a white suit and an emerald satin shirt. Just as they reach the door her father turns and points to Lily, then points to the ceiling and makes exploding-nova motions with his hand and Lily, at the time, understands what this means.

It was a certain kind of cynical innocence they'd had, after the collapse of wide-eyed belief. The contrast had been too much for a lot of the Sixties people, but her parents, too young to have experienced the notion of expectation, danced smoothly into the disco years, their sole error being that they believed in them, her mother humping the office tower like King Kong, her father melting down at a New Age concert, Lily arriving and taking the sad-eyed stares of the alternatively enlightened, her father crying like a teething baby.

She still felt a twinge of guilt at the thought of him sputtering his last in one of the ManorHomes. Lily had been too fiscally freeze-dried to care for him following her mother's death. And so, the ManorHome, one of the ugly restructurings of the late nineties. Better to have died when her mother had, a faulty transfusion statistic that helped spark the counterattack against the Disease. Better to have....

And she realized she was renomemming again, renovating her past until it lined the eyelids of her current vision. She had not learned much since she'd been on the run. Her sum total of practical knowledge, in fact, could be summarized by the epigrams her parents had lived by. Her mother had taught her: 'You can be whatever you want to be if you don't let the bastards get you down.' This from a future epidemic statistic. From her father she had learned: 'Do whatever you have to do to stay alive,' which had almost sounded not dumb until Lily realized it was just another take on her father's anthem, "Stayin' Alive", which had gone on to become one of the consensually Hated Songs. When it was banned from play even on the Golden Oldies station, her father stood naked in the westbound lane outside the Canadian Tire.

What would they think of her now, holed up in a cave, a not-smart idea in itself, given that it was a glacial cave and frozen, given that she had been told by someone she didn't know to wait inside the Angel? Her contact would meet her there, unless of course, her contact was already dispensed with and Lily was freezing up here for nothing. Or for penance. Yes, they would want the penance, too.

The Angel, a shimmering blue glacier on the Cavell mountainside, its wing-span belting the rock face like a massive condor, a two-dimensional seabird smacked against a wall, shadow of a passing spirit.

And a tourist attraction, except now, except this late in the season when only fools would enter the watery mouth and crouch on a Weathermonger blanket. To her parents' edicts, Lily Dalriada had added her own: don't think too much; don't think about it too much; don't dwell on the here and now.

*

Her thoughts, as always, are of Beatrice, of a rainy Tuesday afternoon back in the Lister Apartments. Lily is taking the day off because Beatrice has a cold. They sit together on Beatrice's bed, watching the raindrops slide down the window glass, Beatrice making splashing sounds whenever a raindrop reaches bottom.

— *Mama, are they gone, all gone?*
Fingers fibrillating.
— *Mama, are we happy here?*
Beatrice's clear eyes, the serious questions of a five year- old.
Six.
Lily inhaled sharply.
She had missed her daughter's birthday.

*

Lily had been filling her VoxBox with messages for Beatrice. She couldn't send them directly; too risky. Even sending them from a Memostation in the city was dangerous, which was why she hadn't tried it in Calgary. So she was amassing them, creating a diary for her daughter. A diary! While she was being hunted down? The thought possessed its own classic absurdity, Lily with her portable god carried in cloth from town to town.

Gods from before the steeples fell, when the amulets had offered hope. Now it was just the hollow forms that abounded, the draped officials of the Church of the Survivors.

Ye pays yer money and ye takes yer chances. This is the church and this is the steeple, open the door and....

Lily shuddered.

She pulled her VoxBox from the small backpack. Her fingers were numb. She slid them along the sleek case, back and forth as if she was telling beads.

Here are my fishes, little Bea.

They will swim through secret channels, through the pinholes in the Net.

She began recording:

Sept. 23, 2010
Beatrice:

    Listen to me. We have lived through the trees and
skipping and hopscotch six times now, and wasn't it you
who said the coloured leaves would come back again this year?

    Pointing your determined finger at the green wrappings of
spring, believing in the crisp gold floating of fall leaves?

    And so they have returned and so you are six years old. You
have celebrated your birthday with Anna, and Mama couldn't be
there.

    I'd wanted to make you a special cake with six candles at the
six points of the Hyades. Aldebaran, remember? The blazing eye
of the bull forever facing and charging Orion? You probably don't
remember. It was a long time ago.

    Beatrice, listen, I know you're a big girl now, but you have to
make yourself very small. There, now, hold in all your birthday
feelings. Now send them out, all at once, through the sky, send
them to Mama. I'll catch them, I promise. Now make your wish.
Now hold. Now let it go.

There was so much she wanted to tell her daughter, but where to begin? Beatrice didn't understand why Lily had to leave, or why the Sanitation Commission had moved them from the Lister Apartments. The child didn't like the Hansen Block. It was dirty, crawling with children and vermin. Funding always seemed to stop across the street from the ugly brown rectangles that dotted the outskirts of cities. They had sprung up so quickly following the council consensus, and the forced relocation had begun. It was one way of controlling the Disease, they said. It was the only way to keep the Stigs together.

She could barely remember the transition period, it was so short. They had gone from legislation protecting DNA discrimination to voluntary testing, to pre-employment testing. It was a quick route from there to predisposition counselling, predisposition screening, and the quarantine.

Lily had never told anyone other than Anna that her daughter was a Stig, a product of actual human intercourse. Beatrice had grown up in the Lister Apartments, comfortably accepted by the rest of the residents. And Lily had lied, lied through her teeth, on every form she had had to sign.

> — *Is your child clean?*
> — *Are you clean?*
> — *Have you documents from the Neonatural Institute?*

False documents, false papers provided by Anna, which stated what they desired:

> *Beatrice Dalriada, daughter of Lily Dalriada, conceived at*
> *Neonatural Institute Branch 17, born September 23, 2004.*

Had Lily been married, the semblance would have been closer, a clean mother and a clean father and a child, their own child, yes, but a medically approved one. As it was, officially she had a clean baby, with an assigned father for Christmas and Survivors' Day and the picnic at the Institute.

How could anyone have known? And could she truly blame them for trying to control the spread of the Disease? They couldn't seem to cure it, and it had wiped out so many.

It had split the population.

Lily had chosen to make her child, not to grow it. She had taken Edward into her, ignoring the warnings of the Council and the Sanitation Commission. So the child was a Stig, and now that this was known, she would live a circumscribed life.

But she would not be alone.

For despite all the attempts by the Council, Stig children were being born to women across the country, as men disappeared down alleys in the night.

Edward was gentle, which itself would doom him. Edward was a library serf, digitally transferring chosen information to the Net. He did not get to do the choosing himself, and sometimes he told Lily about the books that didn't make the cut. Florid prose accounts of love, poetry about almost everything, how-to books that referred to resources no longer available. And biographies, lives he would toss into the canvas bin beside him, to be conveyed to the shredder. He swore he could hear voices crying out as they fell.

Poor Edward. He could hardly believe he was in some way responsible for these decisions. Madame Curie? Yes. Bobby Orr? Yes. Edgar Bergen? No. Charlie McCarthy's wooden jaw flapping uselessly.

Edward would sit beside her on the roof, looking through the telescope, speechless in his pain. Sometimes she brought out a blanket and they huddled under it, and one such time he turned to her with his eyes full of words and they performed the ancient ritual. A word or two escaped as they wrestled beneath the stars. Lily heard a questioning "love", but perhaps it was "alive." It was *live* or *love* he grunted as she saw into his eyes, where all the people lived.

It was a bad pulp novel from the last century.

It was a disco dream date from her father's time.

There was a man named Edward who loved his little girl, who would never ever visit her, whom she would never ever know. Instead, his daughter would sit beside someone named Harry who would drone "Silver Bells" to her and then go away until the next time there was a holiday, Beatrice turning away from him and looking at the tree, ringing a small tin bell from her grandmother's time.

— *Teacher says every time a bell rings....*

And none of it was working. Not the Church/State government, not the ManorHomes, not the desperate Hansen Blocks. The unemployment rate, 43 percent, was beyond anyone's control or concern. Lily knew that Beatrice's chances of ever finding a job were nil, especially now that her status was known. What if she cut her finger at work? What if you were next on the toilet she'd just vacated?

*

They used to sit up late in the Lister Apartments watching ancient movies. Her father's collection of old timers, ludicrous love sagas, comical horror films all lovingly transferred as the technology changed, from Beta to VHS to disk to the Net. Beatrice preferred the really old stuff, 70-year-old westerns. She would sit cross-legged on the floor, swaying left and right in her quilted robe, singing "Home on the Range" word for word as the wagon trains pushed on.

— *Mama, is the buffalo that big head from millions of years ago?*
— *That's the tyrannosaurus, Bea.*

Explaining the extinction of the buffalo had been easy. Explaining John Wayne had taken some time.

*

Someone had told the Sanitation Commission about Beatrice. It wasn't Anna. Anna was a friend and, besides, she would have been implicated if she had informed.

No. It must have been one of the Good Neighbours.

Good neighbours make good fences, the garbled wisdom of the billboards.

*

The Hansen Block was cold and poorly lit. Children ran through the halls screaming and hammering on doors. Who knew what went on in the parking lot out back? When Lily and Beatrice moved in, Lily had made her daughter memorize an arm's-length list of rules, new ultimatums that had brought the five-year-old to tears.

— *I can't go on the swings? They're right there!*

A trio of rusty seats and chains over by the dumpster.

Lily, the ogre, with yet another jigsaw puzzle, Beatrice's feet dangling beneath the dining room chair.

It was chaotic and depressing there, but it was also where she met Alex and Giulia, where she first learned of the Underground. Usually, their function was that of self-defence, of warnings to people that their jobs were on the line, or their housing. Or even their children. It was a camaraderie of the dispossessed. At first Lily resisted it.

It had something to do with groups, with joining anything. And yet, the people risking their lives for her right now were a group of these Stigs and outcasts.

She remembered the hospitality clerk in one of the big hotels. He had certainly risked his livelihood hiding Lily.

— *I've been chosen*, she warned him. *Don't you see?*

He did see. And brought food to the tiny alcove near the brooms and cleaning supplies.

— *I've never seen a saint before.*

He said it so humbly, it hurt.

It was through Giulia that Lily had heard the rumours of the other saint, Domenica, the Plague Saint of the other time. Lily had been interested in history even as a child. She had read about Florence, and while her reading was not extensive, the rumours she heard now of the Church's adherence to Florentine policy and, especially, the rumours of the saint, intrigued as much as they unnerved her. She had wanted to ask Giulia more questions; but, too suddenly, she had had to leave.

Anna had approved of Giulia and Alex. And so it was through them that Lily made her escape.

— *Anna will stay with you. Anna will watch you, okay, little Bea?*

And the blow that only a child knew how to deliver.
— *If you don't want me, do I have to go to that daddy, Harry?*

Lily had given Beatrice a red stained-glass fish that had been Lily's grandmother's. Beatrice leaned it up against the window sill and peered through it.
— *It looks like Mars outside,* she said.
And turned her face away from Lily's kiss.

*

Lily peeled back the cover on the hot-pack. Only two left, and they hardly kept her hands warm. This was by far the most foolish move yet. She was alone in a cave, waiting for someone who might be an enemy. Maybe they were all camped outside waiting for her to come out.

Or, why bother? That was it. Let her stay in here and freeze to death. Yes, the body well-preserved, the body sanctified. Maybe this was the way they'd planned it all along. Lily started walking in circles, slapping her mitts together and stamping her feet in a quick march.

Lily's father had believed that if you kept moving — dancing, actually — if you just kept dancing, nothing could catch you. Yet, there was that laundry clerk at the cleaners. She caught up to Jack for two years and only left when he paid her way back to Newfoundland. After the promises and Mona's forgiveness, he would regale his Friday bar crew with stories of how this babe had taken him to the cleaners. Despite the false steps, the bad investments in electronic typewriters and Beta VCRs, he kept dancing.
Lily smiled as she paced.

He was impervious. When punk and post-punk music came on the scene, he closed his door and cranked the disco higher. When his *Rubbermania* Stamp Company drowned in the wake of the computer explosion, he got into men's natural-fit jeans. That was his other joke: he had gotten into young men's jeans. They had looked deliberately strange with the platform heels.
Lily had only seen him miscued once, when he looked at his wife's body through the glass window. He had a face Lily had never seen before, not when he tripped and fell at the Retro Dance Competition, not when his parents overdosed in a mutual suicide embrace.
—*She was the best chick on the floor,* he whispered, nodding at the

spectre behind the glass.

Lily knew how he had felt about the dry-cleaning clerk. So Lily realized he was remembering his wife from back in the glory days. And Lily could see them, once again in their prime, Jack twisting Mona around in what was almost a death spiral. They were so smooth.

Beatrice:
> Everybody was crazy back then. Things were changing so fast, you had to dance your feet off. Grandpa's line.
> You have to understand, Beatrice, that your grandpa never saw himself as ridiculous, or as a grandpa. He never thought these dopey things he did would be what he was remembered for. I have to be careful when I tell you things. What he would have liked you to have known is this: Jack Dalriada believed in parties and dancing. He never hurt anyone intentionally. He loved Mona, your grandmother, jealously and deeply. He truly thought she was the most beautiful thing on earth. He had a not smart head for business. His feet itched but he took good care of them. He had 23 pairs of shoes at any given time. He didn't know why 23. He never thought much about getting old, or of having grandchildren, but he would have loved you very much. He tried not to be a burden when he got old.

Inside the Angel, Lily thought about her childhood. It seemed a funny concern given the situation, but that was the way things went, wasn't it? Nero fiddling while Rome burned, a feeling of peace as you stopped thrashing in the water, a sensation of warmth as you closed your eyes in the snow-bank.

Lily got up again and made her way to the mouth of the cave. It was said that the Angel's wings were over 40 metres thick. Lily could hear the icefalls breaking overhead. She opened her eyes only as wide as slits, and trained them on the path of ascent to the glacier.

You fool.

The quiet hospitality clerk, his face as he gave her the thermal socks.

She felt the Angel rise above her, the thundering shiver of its wings.

— I've never seen a saint before.

Lily pulled the blanket around her shoulders and, for the first time since she left her daughter, allowed herself to cry.

*

It was orange.

She pressed her mitts to her stinging eyes. Concentrate.

Something orange.

A figure was criss-crossing the path. She could catch glimpses of it when the winds died down. The figure was determinedly making its way toward the lake and the glacier.

This was either her contact or her executioner. Or both, she thought, even as she raised a hand in greeting. And she could see the large cracked oil painting in the museum, Saint Apollonia as they are smashing her teeth, Saint Lily welcoming and forgiving her tormenters. Lily's heart pierced by the soldier's sword. Lily's skin scraped with conch shells, curling into ribbons.

"Hello," she calls out. Face your competition. Dance your ass off. There is no other way.

The bearded man, too, lifted his hand in acknowledgement, and it reminded Lily, all at once, of the old westerns Beatrice watched, non-aboriginal men in Hollywood paint saying "How!" with fierce enthusiasm.

"They couldn't find something more uncomfortable?" he asked without change of expression. Who were "they"? Lily stooped to pick up her belongings. "In Calgary," she said, careful not to offer too much. "In Calgary they told me to wait inside the Angel. Uh...I'm Lily."

"Saint Lily," he responded sardonically, as if Lily might somehow be enjoying this experience, might secretly see herself as noble and lofty. She looked sidelong at him. He was checking a pocket watch or a compass. He was of average height with a rounded body and blunted features.

Lily put on her pack. "So, where are we going?"

He said nothing, imagining no doubt that she must think him very stupid if he should tell her their destination. Lily had to remind herself that these people were risking a lot for her.

"We have a long way to go," he said. "Stay with me."

And the two emerged from the Angel's mouth just as the wings turned blue in the late afternoon light.

*

Crying on the corner, "popolo minuto", "spedale", "lazaretto", *as tears flow from his eyes. The dogs are by the Arno. The dogs are down by the river.* Ufficiale del morbo *have arrived in his quarter; they have closed his neighbour's house.*

He holds tight to the bones of a toad in his pocket. He remembers the white wand of this grandfather's time, the walking dead, his grandfather picking his way through the cobbles, a white stick tapping the glistening stones.

He curses his neighbour, afraid the Magistracy will close his street. He swears at the lanzi, *the fugitives from abroad. Surely they have brought this Bad Disease down from the mountain paths to the gates of the city. All through the Valley the Plague Virgin is walking, spreading a black blanket over the Po. The Germans, their hides of buffalo. The soldiers pulling on pants and shirts taken from the houses.*

Wasn't it always the travellers, wasn't it always strangers who brought it to the city? "Bordone, vagabondo!" *he cries. He studies the dab of mercury inside the hazelnut, and rolls it carefully back and forth in his hand.*

Already the family name is in the Grascia Morti, *the ink drying on the words he used to call his daughter.*

MARGHERITA FRANCESCO, di Santa Maria Novella. morto. via Trebbia "P" (pistolenza")

He remembers her eyes, the milky, almost blue tint of the white; the way the iris was ringed with a darker brown than the gentle taupe of the centre. He remembers the pinks of the rims, and the translucence of the lids. When they closed he had to catch his breath as if it was his life that was ending, not hers.

He has never seen the Books of the Dead. He knows only that his child exists there now, in those words, which do not tell how she survived the mal maestro, *the disease of her infant year; or how she balanced proudly on two tiny feet out under the chestnut tree.*

He had consulted his planetary who had read nothing in the stars, no warning that the golden curls would twist so fitfully in fever. The planetary had studied him, had offered alembics, the eyes of lynxes, dried plants gathered during all the lunar phases.

All for nothing. The hazelnut in his hand.
Babbo, babbo.
Sleep, little one. Fare la nanna. *Go to sleep.*

*

They had driven for several hours. Had they doubled back toward Calgary at some point? Were they going to the coast? All Lily knew was that it was dark when they finally stopped.

Lily had never realized that people were this desperate. Rather, that they were this organized in their despair. The so-called Underground was actually a place. There were buildings here; there was equipment. The complex had begun, Lily was told, as a project back in the '80s. A technician from the University of Alberta had designed it as an ecologically-sound retreat, the perfect getaway from the stresses of the high-tech '80s. The stresses of the 80s; Lily had found the thought quaint given what had come later. She remembered how her own parents, too, had seen it this way.

Inside the complex, the top of which was observable from the outside as a series of small raised panels that might have been chicken incubators for all anybody cared, a community existed. The only key to location had been a comment by a woman named Wendy who had said: "Just us and the dinosaurs." Which conjured in Lily some vague reference to the Badlands? A national park? Something from the schoolbooks and archaeology.

"You hungry?"

They provided a meal of vegetables — hydroponically grown, they said proudly — fresh bread, and meat, if she wanted it.

"Hell, this is Alberta." From the years of the beef cattle.

They also had homemade beer.

Lily accepted the food and drink gratefully. She had so many questions but really didn't know how much she was allowed to ask. Did they live here all the time? Were they all Stigs? Or were they outcasts of another kind?

A young boy of nine or so was eyeing her, studying her clothes and the way she was wolfing down the food. Lily smiled at him but he just kept circling.

"Hi," she mouthed between chews.

"You're her," he said slowly, a little puzzled by the vision. "You're not how I thought you'd look."

"Her? Her who?"

"You know, the saint."

Coming from him it sounded strangest of all.

"No...look. I'm just somebody, Lily, I'm Lily and I'm just somebody they picked, I don't know, out of a hat or something. I don't know why!"

She realized her voice had risen; two passing people glanced her way.

"Uh, look, what's your name anyway?"

The boy's expression had not altered throughout the exchange. "Mark," he said. "I'm Mark."

"Mark, what was the name of the man who brought me here? He seems to have disappeared. I wanted to thank him."

"Oh, that's Roland. He can't stay. He doesn't live here."

"So you don't all live here?"

"No," he watched her curiously. "That would be dumb."

The boy was called away by a woman who had poked her head into the room. Lily put her plate aside and went over to the couch. It was rough to the touch and low, but not uncomfortable. Compared to the ice and rock floor, it was great. She felt an undulation of pain move through her head as soon as she leaned back against the arm of the sofa. Lily twisted around and grabbed her knapsack up off the floor. She'd have to see about sending the messages. She stuffed the knapsack beside her and held on to its strap.

Oh, Beatrice.

Are you alone in that cold bedroom? Or has Anna brought you somewhere warm? The thought of Anna comforting Beatrice disturbed Lily despite Lily's gratefulness.

Bea, Bea.

Lily was too tired to record. She needed a rest, just a few minutes. She closed her eyes to the humming of what sounded like large machines.

*

"Lily...Lily, dear. Stay close," her mother cautions.

They have left the car halfway up the mountain and are continuing on foot past the crucifixes and grey stones.

"Look at this," Lily crouches beside the path. There is a tiny white stone with faded writing. An angel's face is spooky in the stone.

"Sssshhh...get back here. That means a baby died."

Lily allows her mother to hold her hand but can't help looking back at the tiny white marker. She watches it until it is as small as a fingernail sticking up out of the earth.

"It's over here," Lily's father says. The family plot. The place where her daddy's family is buried. Her father has told her that the plot has been in the family for years and years and that *his* grandma and grandpa are buried there. And Uncle Mikey from the war. And Aunt Jennie's busted lungs. And now Lily's grandparents, "Mom and Dad", her father says.

They stand, three of them, side by side in front of the bunched up earth. The new names have not yet been added to the Dalriada stone, but there is Uncle Mikey, Sergeant, and there, as always, is Aunt Jennie.

Lily's father is standing very straight and Lily, holding his hand, feels him bending his back up tight the way he does before he dances.

"I still can't believe it," Lily's mother says quietly.

"It's funny," he almost whispers. "They really wanted it to be like the '50s. You know, Dean Martin singing 'That's Amore' or something."

"They didn't fit."

"No, ma'am, they sure as heck did not."

Lily likes it when her father talks like a movie cowboy.

"Thing is, they never understood the '60s. But they tried." He starts to chuckle.

"What?"

"They bought love beads. He wore them with his blue serge suit."

He smiles at this.

And that is all they say.

Lily unlinks her hand and wanders over to the tree that has always been right beside the Dalriada stone. She sits under it and looks at her parents who are weeding around the stone. Her father is wearing the nice suit, the pale green one with the shirt that has flowers. He is in the high boots, too.

Lily wants to go back and look at the stone of the little girl but her mother says no, says that would be in poor taste. The baby belonged to somebody else and, anyway, the stone is so old everybody who knew her was probably dead.

Lily thinks about this in the car on the way home. How it makes it more sad and not less that the baby is alone on the mountain. She thinks about her grandparents, too, and how they drank the stuff that put them to sleep. They were in their nicest clothes, grandma in the pale violet dress, and they went to sleep hugging each other as if they were dolls.

Lily watches a grey squirrel dash back and forth among the skinny trees. When they get home, her mother says, they can make chocolate fondue.

*

Lily was welcome in the complex but never expected she would be able to stay there for any length of time. They would keep her for a couple of days, three at most. Eventually they hoped to be able to spirit her out of the country.

Which confirmed her fears.

"Beatrice...."

Once she was safely away, she was told, they would concentrate on sending her daughter to her.

To where?

Lily had never travelled. Even with official business there were the endless checkpoints, the battery of medical tests, all with no assurance that you would be let in anywhere else. The Disease had shut down the travel industry, and in its wake the TraveLOG-ONs had surfaced, mini or even micro boutiques that offered simple virtual reality programs of trips to Meddy Olde England, a walk along the Great Wall, children picking apples in the Annapolis Valley, peasants harvesting rice in Viet Nam. It was how people saw the world, in either twelve or twenty-two minute segments. Lily couldn't imagine a country full-time.

The news left Lily subdued. She tried reading the information printouts on the table but found she could not concentrate. Then she enquired about sending her messages to Beatrice and was told to wait until Roland returned.

"He's the one to ask. He works in a communications firm."

"Where?"

"If anybody could help you, it'd be Roland."

She was told he would be returning that evening for the general meeting. Lily had no choice but to wait.

Beatrice:
When you were very little Mama promised you
you'd be able to go up in the sky and see the Milky Way.
Remember? How sad you were every morning when the
stars went away?
Mama thinks it's time for an adventure. Anna will
know what to do and she'll help you. In the meantime, I
hope you are brushing your teeth.
I love you, Bea,
Mama

"You're the saint, aren't you?" a pleasant-faced woman spoke as Lily stood under the communal shower. Though the woman was standing beside her, the words were muffled by the water sounds and came to Lily as if she were hearing them in a dream. Lily's hair was slicked flat and formed dark lines across her shoulder blades.

"Look at me. Do I look like a saint?"

A cluster of soap bubbles in her pubic hair. She swirled the cloth over herself, then stepped out from under the water and reached for her towel.

"Listen," Lily added. "I have a question. Why is it some of you —"

She shouldn't have said *you*.

"Why is it that some people actually seem to believe all of this? You —"

She said it again.

"You know the Church. They're all a bunch of Creeders! They don't believe it. Nobody in the Church of the Survivors believes any of this. I don't know what they're trying to do. It won't make anybody believe...but, apparently I'm wrong because look at you! You, out there, people who walk up to me as if I'm a holy person. Me! All I want to be doing right now is kissing my kid and getting the hell out of here. Is that how a saint thinks?"

"I wouldn't know," the woman smiled, not taking her eyes off Lily.

"Well? You guys are supposed to be the enlightened ones, aren't you? Otherwise you'd all be out there in the malls like the rest of them."

The woman paused. "And for you awareness is cynicism?"

And she smiled so sweetly that Lily was taken aback, then she turned and walked away and left Lily watching the outline of her trim buttocks all the way out of the shower room.

*

"Donna Summer," her father said, enjoying the sibilant sizzle. "She was hot, hot, hot. Then, I think, she went born-again."

He said it without bitterness but with the sadness one would feel watching a son break up with a girl the whole family had liked. Then he said, "Wasn't meant to be."

"What wasn't?" Lily asked, straightening up the tiny room, removing *Butterfinger* wrappers.

"Donna, disco. It's like a dream."

"Taking your medicine, Dad?"

The latest round of public heartbreaks, her father naked, painted blue and white, at a Toronto Blue Jays game.

"Dad, you really have to do this. It helps keep things in order."

"I don't know if she stayed born again. Do you ever see anything about her in the paper?" He looked at Lily for an answer. "I mean, what are you called if you go born again and then give it up?"

Lily hated the ManorHomes.

*

She lay on her bunk thinking about her situation. She still didn't know why they had chosen her.

The Church had sprung from the barbecue ashes of the traditional churches which had faltered in the general collapse surrounding the millennium. One or two of the larger denominations had limped along for a while on single-note cries. The spread of the Disease had kept the anti-promiscuous lobby busy, and the lack of jobs and any hope for reasonable futures kept everyone hopping.

But eventually all had given way to fear. Fear and cynicism. Governments lasted months, the population complaining that the only vote they wanted was the vote of NO CONFIDENCE. And so they had taken it. Churches were converted into video halls and arcades, and the faithful, if there were any, were forced to find smaller, less conspicuous accommodation.

Catacombs, Lily thought.

And where am I now? And what was the Angel?

And it had given rise to Ren Bogen. His fatherly visage that never exactly looked at you, a *pater familias* in his dotage; his enraged xenophobia. The man's eyes, Lily nodded. They never photographed a direct gaze. But nonetheless he had been the uniting force.

And so, out of it all had arisen the Church of the Survivors, the 'Church of Forever Today'. Whereas there had been isolation and fear, now there was community — the survivors were brethren, they had made it through the worst of the depression, they had shielded themselves as much as possible from the Disease. They associated only with approved personnel. They had sexual contact with their partners only in the safety of the Net, virtual lover's mouth pressed to the penis of virtual beloved, the fitful body squirm twisting up through fibre optics.

And somehow most people had managed to adapt. They had taken the alien world to heart and tamed and subdued their one little corner of it. Like Milton's Lucifer trying to get used to the new digs, counting on his mind *not to be changed by place or time:*

> *The mind is its own place and in itself*
> *Can make a Heaven of Hell, a Hell of Heaven.*
> *What matter where, if I be still the same*

But they weren't the same, were they?

How to become different, to change into other matter? Where were the catalysts? Chalk dust, the intercom sounding off the soccer scores. Carol and Tony and Debbie and Lily during Thursday afternoon free periods. The Alchemists.

*

Canis sydus morbus praenunciat. *The constellation of the dog will bring the plague.*

Dio, Dio, *head bowed and fist beating breast, candles shuddering in the chill of Santa Maria Novella.*

Dio, Dio, *the animals are falling. The fish on the tongue is putrid and strange, the water smells of rotting wood. Protect your servant, O Father, from the dog in the sky.* Keep the seal of the Public Health Magistracy from the door, and the men of the Magistracy from the dark folds of my body. Let the house remain open, the doors unlocked. Protect your servant, Dio, from the beccamorti, let the sounds of their bells be far away.

And she thinks, now, of the light on the Feast of Saint John, how

*the piazza was sparkling with movement. Golden fabric decorating
the shops, fine silks and ornate brocades. Processions, the clergy led
by saints and angels to the singing of the choirs. And there, there are
the sacred relics and, there, the tall banners of the regions. In the
Piazza della Signoria, gilded towers, so many it is said they number
one hundred, brought on wagons to the square, and on every tower
are likenesses of animals, girls, men, soldiers, horses, rabbits, birds.
And at the moment when the light is changing them almost to flame,
they begin revolving, each one turning slowly so that, even in memory,
she crosses herself and closes her eyes. So strong, the beauty, she
whispers and presses the chip of amethyst in her fist.*

*

There was a ceremony. This surprised Lily. The older members
sat at one long table facing the group. Roland appeared and was
engaged in conversation with one of the elders.

She was calling them elders.

This was very strange. Things were so formal. Weren't these just
the loser-outcasts from cities and towns across the country? Then Lily
reminded herself that she was a saint. Strange didn't begin to cover it.

"We would like to welcome a friend this evening. Lily is on a
journey and we will do everything we can to make it a successful one
for her."

Faces turned in her direction and Lily nodded and smiled
awkwardly.

"Some of you have taken the designation to heart, and we will not
judge you for it. Your consciences are your own. We want you to
know, Lily, that those of us who do not believe in your sanctity are in
every way committed to maintaining your safety. In fact, in a curious
way, we are possibly more committed.

"You will find no infighting here, no forced statements such as you
find in the State Church. Here, those of true belief live alongside the
remainder of us, united as we are in our stand against the Creeders.
Though your stay will be brief, we will make it as comfortable for you
as possible."

That was it. They moved on to other business: supplies, delegation
of duties. No word about her daughter.

"You can take my bedroom." The woman from the shower. "You'll
be warm enough there and you can use my clothes if you want to."

"I need to know about my daughter. Doesn't anybody have contact with — "

"You'll want to ask Roland. You know, the man who brought you here. He keeps us plugged in."

Roland.

Where was he? He'd been standing up beside the long table. Now he was gone.

"He'll be back," she said, before Lily could ask. "If you like, I could take you to him."

*

Beatrice drawing a picture of a tiger, scaring herself with its ferocity.

— *Just don't make the teeth,* Lily advises.

— *I have to, Mama. They're there.*

Beatrice's entire being balancing on the fleshy pad of her hand as she draws the fur around the tiger's neck.

The child used to wonder about the stars, the real ones visible on good nights when the satellite advertisements were orbiting elsewhere. Lily had known little about stars, so she had dutifully gone through the books.

Mister Copernicus. Doctor?

Mister Galileo.

Beatrice had liked Galileo. She said he sounded like a sheriff in a western. So Lily had played "Galileo and John Wayne" with her daughter, Lily sidling up to an imaginary bar and asking:

— *Ahm'a lookin' for a man goes by the name of Galileo.*

And Beatrice with perfect timing:

— *That's Sheriff Galileo to you, pad'ner.*

The stars had held them many an evening. They had freed Lily somehow. They were so old, or perhaps that was the wrong way to look at it. They had been there for so long. Her parents had walked home after dancing the night away under these very stars. Her grandparents. Lord, her great-grandparents had crooned love songs under them, Bing Crosby, Frank Sinatra.

They freed her from the here and now, which was always a gift to Lily. And they did it without the blank erotica of the virtual world. Just Lily and Beatrice, a few thumbed books and an inexpensive telescope on the top of the Lister Apartments. Most of the time they couldn't see anything at all, but they imagined they saw this planet, that nebula. It was its own world, eyepiece in place, the universe up close and personal.

Beatrice had understood so much at a nearly age. She had known that searching for stars was more important than finding them. She'd known instinctively that this was something bigger than a hobby.

And now, what would she comprehend now? What would she figure out now, the telescope still on the roof of her old home?

— *This town ain't big enough for both of us.*

John Wayne, always the bad guy in Beatrice's westerns, calling out the Sheriff in front of the entire saloon.

— *Whaddya gonna do about it, pad'ner?*

And John Wayne, Lily, makes her move and Sheriff Galileo is faster, and Lily falls to the bar-room floor once again.

When the new technology split the population Lily found herself on the losing side. She had never been especially fond of machines. Her father had given up trying to teach her how to program the VCR. Her mother talked and typed into machines at work, but then had spent her last days hooked up to them, at their mercy. And by the time Lily hit the so-called work force, the lines were drawn. You either had it or you didn't.

Lily didn't and cleaned office buildings, ticketed dry-cleaning — just as her father's "babe" had done. There were artists digging ditches, drill-press workers cleaning windows. Had it ever been this clear? It was feudal except that now the serfs were educated, or cultured, or what would pass for cultured in another time. And they were caught in this time warp where the very things that had been valued for eons were now peripheral curiosities.

Could you interact? Were you wired, hooked up?

The phrases had changed but the message was the same: could you freely and without reservation plug into a giant information system that would swallow you? And, in Lily's case, could you stop renomemming, living in the past, dragging that decaying corpse everywhere you went?

Lily had failed to make the millennial transition. So many had, it had become a joke. Rubbing an elbow or holding a head. Yeah, my MT is bothering me. Gotta do some TM for my MT.

Yeah.

So it was with no small degree of foreboding that Lily surveyed the computer room in the complex. Roland was there, moving from machine to machine, typing in the odd command, voice-activating others. He seemed at home in the place.

"They said you might be able to get me some information," Lily said.

Roland said nothing, but motioned for her to follow him.

It was impossible to explain the sense of detachment Lily felt standing among the hardware. Was she a peasant rubbing her eyes and gawking up at the spire in Rhiems, in Cologne? Was there any love thick in her womb as she swayed before the mainframe? Impossible to explain how lost they had all become, how the brothers of friends had quietly expired in unpainted rooms, opening cans with jagged thrusts, staring at cardboard reprints of the Taj Mahal. Alone. In the ManorHomes, Grandparents talking to soap opera characters; children in daycare boot camps, bright colours flying on the drab grey afternoons. Beatrice watching the ancient movies, laughing with the long-dead at the stories of another century.

All of it gone, the wartime dance hall, Benny Goodman's clarinet catching the light as the soldier pulls his girl closer, close, baby, I can't get enough of you. The hobo trains, the horse and buggy, Lily's great-grandmother tobogganing down a mountain in Montreal, playing with other immigrant girls who arrive off the boats.

> *Ashes, ashes,*
> *We all fall down.*

And then running-boards, Dillinger, and Jimmy Cagney, the fast machines and the faster machines, and then the Disease and the fireworks, Lily twenty-eight years old when the millennium clicks over, standing on a rooftop with a group of drunken revellers, the sky ablaze with colour and light, and Lily holding up a drink to no one in particular, to the sky, toasting how strange by mere timing of birth, how silly, there in her shiny red hat, how strange to be the one who had to say goodbye to a world.

"You don't like it here," he observed.

"What do you mean? Everyone has been...." What was the word? "Marvellous." No, that was not the word. "Everyone has tried to make me comfortable."

Which was true.

"I meant *Here*."

Lily looked at him, trying to catch the inflection.

"What choice have I got?"

"Any number."

"Oh, right. Yeah, well, for some reason those TraveLOG-ONS have never done it for me. I just don't think you can see a place in 22 minutes. And those other things — "

She was referring to the more free-form VR, to the erotica and the arcades.

"Those stick-figures on Mars, those spread-eagled hallucinations who look just like your swim coach...."

"Those pixels are somebody's true love."

He said it in all earnestness.

"Well, not for me. Not one of the TraveLOG-ONS can take me to the southernmost stars. Sure, it can take me to Cuba, where, funny, there always seems to be music and dancing, but I don't get to see Alpha Centauri, or Hadar, or Canopus."

"Actually, you probably can."

"It's not Real!"

The machines hummed. Lily could feel them through the floor. They were beautiful; or, she believed that Roland thought they were beautiful.

"You aren't a saint."

His face so grave, but a twinkle in his eye.

"What the hell is a saint? I want to hear from my kid. Is there anything you can do?"

"I've been cruising the waves for you. Haven't spotted anything yet."

"She would have tried. They would have by now!"

"I just said I haven't found it yet. They would have to be a little careful, don't you think?"

Lily hated this. She might as well be tied to the tracks or sitting in a jail cell waiting for her gang to bust her out.

"Wait, here's...here's something, I think."

Lily scrambled to the screen.

"Here it comes."

Lily held her breath.

Mama, Mama,

We were singing and I got red mitts for winter. There's a book about animals and some clay to make things. We were trying to sing loud, so you could hear us, but only a lady with a baby down the hall heard us. We got our Big Eye back from the

*other place. We set it up. We can't see as good as before, but we
can see. I'm bringing my posse, Mama.
Love,xxxxxxxxx Galileo xxxxxxx*
   P.S. You know who helped me write this.

Lily put her hand up to the screen. Roland was silent for a few
moments, then he said quietly, "She sounds okay. I don't think I
should print it out. You understand?"

Lily nodded. She was grateful for this. It was pathetic.

"Roland, do you ever wonder what it was like before?"

"Before?"

"A long time ago. Or not even so long. The 1940s, the '50s. Or not
even that long. You realize that my own parents wouldn't even
recognize this world?"

"That's progress!"

A line Lily knew. It had become the angry cry of a small group that
in her parents' time would have been called 'Back to Earthers.' Now
they were not called anything at all, although the rumour was that
they were feared by the Church.

That's progress. But Roland?

"You? You're...you're at the centre of...."

"Whoa!"

Why did he sound like one of Bea's cowboys?

"I didn't say anything but a phrase. And I'm at the eye of the storm
because I prefer it there, because believe it or not it's calmer than out
on the rim."

"So you're not —"

" — going to answer that, no."

Roland worked in what Lily could gather was a highly sensitive
area of the information industry. He lived in the city and came here
only occasionally. He helped trouble-shoot the equipment, and he
offered advice on operations. And he knew, it appeared, far more
than he let on.

Lily couldn't help herself, and asked, "Is it dangerous?"

He responded indirectly. "You learn to embrace incompetence
and system failure. The larger the system, the bigger the holes."

Lily smiled and added, "That's progress."

She felt comfortable with this quiet, aloof man. Maybe it was all
those westerns Bea had forced on her. Taciturn or tongue-tied, he still

said more than most people out there.

Out there. This was how isolation sounded.

"Okay, I have some information that you're going to have to see. I've been monitoring the search and the statements by the Council and the Commission. You should know."

Was how he put it. Lily nodded. She sat on the stool, stretched her legs out before her and said, "Shoot."

Pad'ner.

They knew about Toronto. And Calgary. They were aware of her flight from responsibility, her illegal movements across quarantine zones. They were intent upon finding her.

Roland displayed a document gleaned from church files. It outlined the reasons Lily had been chosen, the necessity of finding a saint from Lily's region, an area recently hard-hit by the Disease. It was about representation. The document drew the official's attention to historical precedents where faith and hope had been restored after the canonization of a local holy person.

"I'm not a holy person."

It acknowledged the shortcomings of the choice, reminding the official that the truly worthy were exceedingly rare. It pointed to the demographics, the 'random but inevitable feel' of the choice. It spelled out her name: LILY DALRIADA. It mentioned Beatrice, the unfortunate stigma that had gone undetected until the choice had been made public. It was too late to alter it now, and it had in fact proven fortunate because now the Stigs could have their own saint, and perhaps this wasn't such a bad thing. Perhaps it would help keep the Stigs in line.

"Stig Saint," Lily mouthed.

The larger the system, the bigger the holes.

Roland had said this as a prayer. And Lily, Saint Lily, was beginning to understand. Information was everywhere. You could not hide, except perhaps in the glut of information itself. Roland had stocked the Net with information, crazy things: appearances she had made, people she had healed.

"What are you trying to do? I'm in enough trouble already!"

"It's got to be this way. Pretty soon there'll be sightings of you everywhere. Pretty soon I'll be seeing you myself."

Embrace confusion.

Lily read over his shoulder the eyewitness account he had just dictated. Lily watched her name change into something holy.

"There's more."

Roland called up another document. It wasn't a declaration or even a memo. It looked to be part of a scholarly paper. It spoke of the Bad Disease, of the need for a local saint to quell anxiety and to foster hope in the middle of the plague.

Lily paused. "The plague?"

That was the first time they had called it that.

Roland pointed to the screen then scrolled down. Lily saw the date. 1633.

"What's this?"

"History," he shrugged. "Research."

"Was this in with that other stuff?"

Roland nodded, his eyes on the screen.

*

Beatrice's finger moving across the night sky of her cardboard Star Finder.

Aldebaran, the Eye of Taurus, the glare as it charges the giant Orion. Aldebaran, the follower, pink glow in the cool late autumn sky, its light is an old man, seventy years in the coming. Its light is already in the past when it arrives, hundreds of trillions of miles, the light of decades and decades ago; it is here, it shines, but what we see is what is past.

*

Non nacque al tempo, *the woman sobs into a linen cloth, the tiny baby closed and pink, dark bud still on the vine, the* maestretto *hanging between her legs.*

Afterward, the cord severed, the infant placed in the box that she has kept her bracelets in, the woman rocks herself and moans, her hand across her eyes, non nacque al tempo, *not at the right time, while Galileo's planets move heretically overhead.*

*

"It's a world," Roland said at last. "It's rebuilt history. I finally get to see some."

"What?"

But he wasn't listening. His eyes reflected the bright glare of the screen.

Rebuilt history. Was that like renomemming? Lily had been doing that for years.

*

She felt herself being rocked, her arm, somebody was holding her arm. Edward, his way of cradling her, making her forget the blare of the neighbour's entertainment system, his touch erasing lines from her face, pain from her shoulders, removing all doubt and age until she is as young and light as a girl in a swing under an oak tree, flying high, her fingers linked with the chain link chain, link chain link chai —

"Wake up, Lily. Come on! Time to move!"

Her mother, dressed for work, rousing Lily before heading to the tower. Lily, all of seven, rubbing her eyes and focusing on the dark cheeks and lips, the stark grey business suit, the padded shoulders, to match her mother's puffy eyes.

"Wake up, Lily. It's time to go."

Lily put her hand to her eyes and shook her head slowly.

The woman's hand was still on her shoulder.

"Sorry I startled you. Roland says it's time to go."

Lily nodded and was out of bed before what was being said actually hit her. She had to go some place further from Beatrice.

"You can take the heavy sweater," the woman said.

Lily turned to thank this woman who had been good to her since she had arrived and found the woman's head bowed as she spoke.

The van was windowless. Lily sat cross-legged in the back on the floor and felt her legs stiffening in the cold. She had been moved so quickly there had been no time to thank anybody. She had wanted to talk to Roland about sending another message through to Beatrice.

Where were they going now? She was afraid of the coast. It meant the last stop, one way or another. If she was lucky, they would be able to get her out of the country. Lucky, leaving her child, leaving her country and going off the continent? She couldn't even imagine they would get her in down south where the controls were tighter.

As a child she had listened to her grandparents talk about how they travelled across Canada in search of summer employment; students, baseball teams, young beatniks out on the highways, hitchhiking with friends to the mountains to work in the resort hotels. Perhaps her grandparents had travelled this road, they must have, snaking through the Rockies. Or slumped back in train seats and watched a country go by, the moving background scenery in an old western.

Sheriff Galileo, badge of Aldebaran, nodding at people from his veranda as he kicks back in his chair and his spurs graze the floorboards.

"Ma'am."

Dust moves down main street.

A touch of his hat and a glance to the heavens.

Lily wished there was a window in the back of the van.

*

— *Mama, Mama, look!*

Beatrice's face registering horror and awe as she cranes her neck back further. The dome of the planetarium glows with the darkest blue light, stars reflected in her eyes. The show is called "The Winter Sky" and appears three times daily on the dome.

Beatrice shrieks and points. She thinks she has seen a shooting star.

— *Mama, Mama!*

Rocking back in her seat.

*

Where was Lily? There was that stop they made to fuel up and now she had a feeling they were heading back east. She pulled the blanket more tightly around her shoulders.

"Well, it's not great, but it's safe for now."

And freezing. Everywhere they took her to was freezing. How could this place be colder than the Angel?

"You won't be here long. Just keep your chin up."

A tiny window.

Lily scanned her new domain.

"How long since this has been used?"

Her companion toed at something on the floor. "Don't know. Since the end of it, I guess."

Lily had seen the outline against the inky sky as she got out of the van. At once imposing, at once comforting, she supposed, in another time. The spire was almost jagged, obviously intentional, a peak leading up to God. The huge doors were several centimetres thick.

I have bats in my belfry, she thought, and only smiled the first time she muttered it. The church was empty. It had stood, as so many others, solitary and silent. The Church of the Survivors had taken over many former churches and cathedrals but, of course, there had been no real need to use all of them. They would have been demolished except there was no public money for such things. It was like those pictures Lily had seen of the old wars, of the communist bloc countries, trees growing through the rooftops of bombed-out buildings, a family living in the front half of a house because the door from the kitchen led to a back half which no longer existed.

Skeletons. Or husks. All over the landscape.

When Lily was a child the churches were open. True, they'd been fading due to scandal and demographics. But she still remembered, parents in tow, pushing up to the front to see the statues and smell the candles and hear the bells after the final Christmas blessing was given.

Now Lily sat down next to the portable generator and opened a can of kernel corn. The wind moaned outside, and Lily wondered where she was.

*

Cranberries popped with little gusts of wind, like the water that shot through a hole in the ice when Lily pressed her foot on the slippery pane.

There was eggnog. Nutmeg. Rum.

They passed around chestnuts and hot mushroom squares.

She sat before the tree examining the bottommost ornaments, the ones that were always ignored, the ones she supposed were up for sacrifice to her grandmother's old tabby, Primrose.

A very old ornament, "one of the first plastic ones", with a red and white Santa twirling inside a clear plastic ball. Then the Czech hand-blown glass violin. The cello. The tuba. Why weren't these up higher on the tree? Lily watched the mute orchestra as the lights played across the surfaces. She would have to talk to her grandmother about this.

"God Rest Ye Merry, Gentlemen."

They all sang.

They sang tidings of comfort and joy.

"Il est né, le Divin Enfant."

And only her grandfather knew all the words. He had sung in a choir as a boy and "Goddamnit, you knew your hymns."

There was always singing. And the cold walk, boots scrunching up the street on Christmas Eve, Uncle Jake humming something to himself, Aunt Tina giggling, all of it muffled under fur or down, and grandmother and grandfather leading the way, past the annual display of lights.

— *I like the way he brought them up the side.*

— *Better than last year.*

— *Same as last year.*

Up the long windy street to the playground and the manger scene on the back of a flatbed truck. The manger made of planks, the hay *real* hay, the figures painted every year to hide the annual chipping and fading. Mary with the red lips. Joseph looking startled yet again. Jesus frozen, frozen naked, arms outstretched in the direction of the lawn-ornament lambs.

And then the best voice, curiously a different voice every year, leading the group back home with a solo.

"*O Holy Night,*
The Stars are brightly shining"

And Lily pushing up the wool rim of her toque and squinting the cold from her eyes to see the stars up there, brightly shining.

*

They had picked and chosen what to take through the invisible door and they had chosen incorrectly. Girls and boys with interactive games, the games playing with one another, not with the children; hand-held hair dryers; shower massages; voice-activated lamps that turned on when you spoke to them; room deodorizers that plugged all the seasons into your socket; and sanitary pads that welded to your panties and held eight litres of liquid.

Armed yet cowed they approached the door. Ahead of them was everything, behind them the last of the years. They weren't special people, this government clerk, that baker of *Wonder Bread*, yet they one by one marched through the door and left the twentieth century.

Lily had watched the fireworks, but all she saw in the lights was the long window and the fluorescent band behind her mother's body, and all she heard between the rippling explosions was her father's voice chanting, "You Should Be Dancing".

Lily peered out the high belfry window at a city. A town? She was hungry and the cold pressed against her face.

"*In the bleak mid-winter"*

Beatrice. Crying Beatrice from a cold dark tower.

What can he do against the poison? His wife weak with child or the Bad Disease. Perhaps it is only another child, he thinks. Perhaps.

Like the others, he stands in the Duomo, the church of Santa Maria del Fiore, waiting for a miracle. Will it come in this new powder they whisper of, this contraierba he has heard about? The Magistracy has some; perhaps he can procure a little.

Placing it in the damask sack and wrapping it around the neck of his wife.

She will wear it next to her heart.

She will be warm with it there on her heart.

Oil of red dog. Myrrh. Nutmeg. Peony seeds. Rue seeds. And more. Things that are mysterious, strange to his ears. Incense from Palestine. Yes. Per piacere.

Crushed, pounded, powdered, a miracle, a mound of dust around her thin throat.

"The scab is black, the ulcer is black and liquid. Swollen."

He has paid the money, all of the scudi he has left. The barber-surgeon swears his wife won't be moved. His wife, her expression as the barber-surgeon bloodlets her, eyes searching her husband's face. The smallest of nods to reassure him, to remind him of her hands when he and she were fifteen years old and they climbed the hill to the olive trees.

The medicines have caused the baby to come. Non nacque al tempo. Her skin has turned inside out. There is only this small dead thing.

The blood flows from her ankle. The bloodletting is complete. The bubo is lanced, his wife's face as she faints from the heat and the fumes.

The light outside Santa Maria del Fiore is soft like the light on her face as she sleeps. He has not slept in a very long time. He crosses himself and approaches. He has come this time to see the doors. He wishes to touch Ghiberti's doors. Was it Michelangelo who called them the Gates of Paradise?

With these hands he has held the body of his unborn baby. A little chestnut still in its shell. With these hands he has wiped the sweat from his wife's face and chest and cleaned the blood from around their child. He wants to touch the doors with these hands, touch The

Gates of Paradise.

*

"Well, well..." a voice came at her. "Some defence."

And he was there before she could even rise from the mat.

"Who are you?" brushing the hair from her face, Lily trying to sound defiant.

"Let's just say I'm a friend you haven't met yet."

He sounded ugly, gravel on the vocal cords.

"A fr...are you moving me already? What's happened?"

"Nice view from here, Rapunzel.... Right, Rapunzel?"

He reached for her and Lily pushed his arm away.

"Oh, baby, baby, let down your hair...."

"I'm...I'm a saint! I'm a chosen saint!"

He smirked then chuckled. "Oh, I know who you are. As I said, I'm a friend. Good fences make good neighbours."

She eyed him coldly, her body now in a full crouch.

"So, you've found me."

"And right here in church, too."

"What's it to be then?" Lily moved to the left, up against the wall. "How are you going to deliver me? Headless? Armless? They've told you by now."

He let out a high-pitched squeal.

"As I TOLD you, I'm a friend. I'm supposed to bring you along and that's all. But there's no reason we can't be nice to each other, is there?"

The grin was worse than the laugh.

Keep dancing. Her father's big platform shoes. He grabbed for her again. "You like it, eh? Stig maker!"

The two-footed kick knocked him flat. Lily fell back, too, but quickly recovered. She stood up and waited. He did not come at her again.

She took small steps over to him. Out cold. He had hit the stone floor with some force. Lily checked his pockets. He had no papers, nothing on him but a rabbit's-foot key-chain that held two keys. A car! She looked out the high window but could see nothing below.

Rapunzel.

Where was she? She couldn't stay here now.

She packed her blanket and took out her flashlight. She was about to start down when she stopped and turned the generator on automatic. Without it, the man would freeze to death.

The dim beam of the flashlight made haloes on the stone wall as she wound down the stairs from the belfry. Inside, the church again engulfed her. She was inside one of the blue whales she had seen in a TraveLOG-ON. The world moved outside the whale's eyes.

Lily pushed on the door. There was an agonized groan as the wood complied. It opened about thirty centimetres and Lily squeezed through.

She was struck by the clean beauty of the night. There were no house lights on in the distance, only street lights. It must be very late, she thought. Very early. Three cars were parked halfway up the street. Two were snow-covered, one was clear.

Lily looked left and right and then ran and skidded toward the vehicle. The key fit into the lock but it didn't matter since the 'friend' had left it open. Lily scrambled in.

It had been years, *years* since she'd driven. When she was sixteen her mother had insisted she learn how to drive. "Then you won't have to depend on boyfriends or husbands" — she gave Lily's father the nod — "to take you everywhere."

Lily put the key in the ignition. The engine turned over.

Thank you, mother.

It was freezing. Lily checked the gauge. Half-full. She could get somewhere on that. But where? Lily pointed her car in the direction of town and drove.

*

The sadness and solemnity of the voices. She hears them, circling the church as haloes around the heads of the priests and acolytes. If she remains still enough the voices enter her perfectly and completely and she becomes part of the sadness and pain.

Outside and down the crying streets she hurries, looking neither this way or that, but making her way along the via dei Vecchietti. At the corner of the via degli Strozzi she stops and looks up. It is there, always, watching and laughing, the Devil perched on the palace wall. Devil's Corner. Why did she not avoid it? Why did she force herself time after time to pass by this way and witness the bronze grimace. It has always been here, this emblem of the Devil, just as this has always been the Devil's Corner. As a child, dancing and singing in the street below the personage. Dio. Children. Children who know so little.

Two men walk by, their feet shuffling quietly. They speak in low tones, and she hears the name Galileo. She looks up just as the belly of the statue tightens.

*

They could probably trace her with a finger as if she were a bug picking its way across a door screen. A ladybug in hot red with polka dots, fierce false eyes that wouldn't fool them for a minute. They knew where she was. Surely they would know where Beatrice was, too? Anna could alter a few files but she did not have access to the entire system. Lily pulled the car over under a streetlight and tugged at the pocket of her jacket. She spoke into the VoxBox:

> *Beatrice:*
>
> *How are you? Oh, Bea, Mama misses you.*
>
> *Just this morning I was thinking about how it was time we had an adventure together. Maybe looked at the stars or something. We could make hot chocolate and pack sandwiches and go to a high place and watch the winter stars. Would you like that? So would Mama. Maybe Anna would like to come too. Could you imagine all of us there, dancing and turning cartwheels on a hillside?*
>
> *Well, you'd have to do the cartwheels.*
>
> *When Mama was little, your Grandma and Grampa took me to see some fireworks one summer. We stood on a hill overlooking a river valley. For some reason, most of the people were in the valley. There were only a few of us up on the hill. When the fireworks started the sky flashed off and on like a camera, like an old-fashioned camera, the kind in the movies, and for a second you saw everyone below and then — poof! — they disappeared. They were there and then they were gone. They looked like people from long ago. That's what I thought then. That they were the people from long ago.*
>
> *Bea...brush your teeth, okay?*
>
> *Mama loves you. I love you.*

The first place she would go would be to a Memostation or to a phone booth that was equipped. It didn't much matter where after that. She drove through the quiet town.

Over there would be where the chained dog would sit, day in and day out, and, there, the cat in the window. The pets would watch the street and wait for nothing to happen. No milk trucks at five a.m., bottles clinking up the walk. No bread aroma seeping from the building down the lane. No mail-man hefting his sack of letters from aunts and uncles, dropping hand-written bits of lives through the slot while people stood by their windows waiting until it was appropriate to go racing to the door to scoop up the letters. And people...daydreaming, yes, but no dreams that meant long journeys, no idle kisses in the school-yard or the playground, bare winter tree pressing into your back as he leans you up against the trunk, and holds you so close in the cold. No dreams of Tibet, of the Australian outback. Dreams when you are ten years old and skating on a pond behind your house.

The world everywhere and nowhere.

Lily saw the light for the automated Memostation and pulled over. This was foolish, but it was not. If they were going to come for her anyway, why was she hiding? Lily inserted her code and sent the message directly.

Here I am, you bastards.

Here I am, Bea. Mama's here.

She touched the terminal as if she were reading Braille.

*

A singer on the corner of the via Matteo Palmieri. One of the old singers, he regales three or four men with storie, *the* cantari *coming one after another as the men nod their appreciation. Yet another verse, sad or funny. The men grunt their approbation. Down the street, Palmieri's Farmacia del Canto alle Rondini, Swallow's Corner. Go to the Swallow's Corner. Perhaps he will have* contraierba, *potions against the Bad Disease.*

A child runs along via dell'Orinolo, a momentary flash of green, pale cheeks bloodless against the grey sky. He slows, a stutter of movement, and as he shifts his face becomes the white afternoon light on the water.

*

She was free. This was what it meant. She drove to the centre of town and saw a diner with the light on. At this hour? Lily parked the car. At least she might find out where she was. Everybody looking for her probably knew.

She stamped her feet on the stoop outside and yanked open the storm door. Aluminum. God, she hated aluminum. Inside, a woman was pouring the remains of one pot of coffee into another pot. The clock behind the woman's head said four forty-five. There were three other people in the place, two men sitting at one end of the counter and a woman in a large felt hat sitting alone at a booth by the window.

Lily nodded to the waitress and sat at the other end of the counter. The men glanced her way.

"Hi...uh, coffee, please."

The waitress flawlessly eased a mug under the overturned pot, pouring Lily coffee from the old batch.

"Eaton?"

Lily was puzzled.

"Eatin'?" the woman repeated.

"Oh...well, are you cooking at this hour?"

The woman evidently regarded this as banter.

"I'm always cookin', honey. Just ask these folks here."

Who looked over and acknowledged the waitress on cue, all of which took Lily aback. She wasn't sure why, only that it might have been a scene from one of the old gangster movies.

"Uh...I'll have a grilled cheese sandwich, if that's okay."

The waitress turned without speaking and went around back to the kitchen.

"You need cream?" The man closest to her asked. He wore a plaid jacket and a day's growth of beard. He lined up the container and skidded it along the counter top in her direction. Lily stopped the projectile and waved a hand his way. The oil product sloshed back and forth in the lidded pitcher.

"New 'round here."

This was the conversational one.

"Uh...yeah. Passing through."

She shouldn't have said that. Nobody 'passed through' towns. This got both men interested and Lily could sense the woman behind her leaning in.

"Well...yeah. I don't live far. Over —"

" — over St. Marian?"

"Yeah, St. Marian."

"Any trouble getting through?"

Lily shifted on the stool. "You know, the usual."

"Who you working for?"

A natural question. Without an approved purpose, how would she travel?

"Nobody."

They stared.

"I mean, I got fired. My boss. You know. Slave labour, slave driver."

An appreciative nod.

"How about you?" Lily countered.

The men looked at each other.

"We don't work," they said in unison, just as the waitress returned with Lily's sandwich. "We none of us here work. Just Martha." A loving grin at the waitress.

"I been catering to you strays for too long. Think I'm gonna go me exclusive. Serve that clientele uptown."

Uptown meant working.

"You a stray, too?" Martha pointed.

Lily shrugged and then nodded. A stray, an outcast. You bet.

"So, I guess I won't be getting paid for the sandwich and coffee, then?"

It hadn't occurred to her. Lily had no cash. You didn't need cash as long as you worked, just your company code.

"I'm...I'm sorry, I just —"

"She just got fired," the plaid man explained. "She's kind of getting used to it, right?"

He smiled a real smile.

Lily gave him one back. "That takes some doing. I mean, without the company code — "

"You'll get by," Martha interrupted. "Look at Medley and Bob, here. You'll see. There are lots of places like this," she motioned to the diner. "It's hard at first."

"It was for me," Medley said.

"And me," Bob grunted.

Lily heard a voice behind her, a soft female voice. "Without the code, you are alone. Nobody watches out for you. They don't even know you're alive."

Was it a lament? Or a prayer?

"You are valueless. They forget all about you."

Lily examined the words carefully and followed them to their source. The woman continued looking out the ice-crusted window and said nothing more.

Lily bit into a pickle.

The bigger the system, she thought.

She asked them how they lived. Some had remnants of family, although this proved to be no guarantee of any help.

"My brother hoiked me out of his garage. Said he might be able to sell it to the city," Medley said.

"Sell it as what?"

"I don't know. A shelter. Firewood. I don't know."

They had friends. They bartered. They exchanged food for work, household objects for a place to sleep. Medley and Bob were luckier than most, having been drawn into a group of five other people who were renting an old house in the slums. Lucky because they had found such a house. Lucky because none of them had been branded Stig or Stig Lover. As bad as the slums were, they were better than the Hansen Blocks.

"But what if you get sick?"

She hadn't specifically meant the Disease, but that was how they took it.

"If we get sick, we die," Bob said simply.

"Not in MY restaurant," Martha grinned.

This was morbid.

"Nobody in our immediate neighbourhood has died in three months."

"So what are you saying?"

"I'm saying," Medley shrugged, "that nobody has died in three months."

Lily waved to the men as they left the diner. It was stupid to feel sad, to feel anything, on their departure. The silent woman by the window did not acknowledge their leaving, but Lily felt she had also taken it in. She had been observant.

Too quietly observant.

Lily picked up her coffee, which Martha had continued to refill, and walked over to the woman's booth.

"Mind if I join you?"

The woman twisted her face even further away, but her hand motioned for Lily to sit. She was young, but between the hat and her avoidance of Lily's gaze, it was hard to get a good look at her.

"Lot of snow," Lily ventured.

The woman said nothing.

"I mean, for this time of year. For this region." How the hell did Lily know that? What an idiot!

"The snow – " the young woman said faintly, " – is very peaceful. Is – merciful."

She offered up the little word.

The left side of the woman's face, which was all Lily could see, softened at this mention.

"When I was a child, my sister and I played in the snow."

She was scarred. Lily could see that now. The Disease? Lily shifted. The woman saw this and faced her directly.

"We all have something, here," she said. Then she added, "Even you."

Lily stared.

"Don't you ever wonder why they can't find a cure?"

"Who are you?"

There were rings on both hands, beautiful stones and settings. Lily didn't know why she was noticing this.

"You want to see Roland?"

Lily sat up straight.

"Who are you?"

"Who I am is not important. Who Martha is...I find that important. Who *you* are has, ironically, become important."

"How do you know Roland?"

"He will have arrived by now. Come with me."

She stood up. Lily could see that, although once lovely, she was both scarred and slightly stooped.

"Come."

An upstairs apartment four blocks away. The woman, whom Lily figured couldn't be any older than she was, laboriously climbed the wide stairs, favouring her right side. A large tapestry bag hung from her shoulder. Lily would have offered to carry it but felt that, somehow, this would be insulting.

There was a band of light under the door. The woman poked around in her bag for keys but the door opened and Lily was once again looking at Roland.

"Well," he said to Lily. To the woman he offered a quick but heartfelt hug. He helped her with her coat and bag. Lily stood apart from them and let her eyes wander around the apartment. A real little home: portraits, photographs, wax fruit in a bowl. The dishcloth had a basket weave pattern that Lily remembered from her childhood. She was instantly comfortable and smiled at Roland and Margaret, which was woman's name, and took her jacket off and placed it by the chair with her pack.

Margaret switched on a lamp in the sitting room. All three of them sat down and Roland led the conversation. He needed the details of the belfry incident. Lily was amazed he had found out so quickly. Amazed but not amazed. Her attacker had quickly revived and informed his superiors.

"I caught their message coming in."

"You should have killed him," Margaret hissed. "Why didn't you?"

Lily felt her stomach knot.

"I thought I had at first. He...hit his head. And I left him like that."

"So he's back on the job an hour later. Wonderful."

"Margaret, she's new to all this. And she's a saint."

"Yeah, right."

It was almost dawn, too late to move Lily. She would have to spend the whole day in Margaret's apartment before moving the following night. "Not a word, understand? This place is always empty when I'm at work."

She was to be taken into the eye of the storm. Into the information jumble itself. It was a risk, to put her so near the source and count on them not to look in their own backyard. It was a giant risk to put her under the protection of....

Bernie Difiori, Communications Techno-Illusionist, purveyor of dreams for the blissful bride and groom, sole owner of *Magical Mystery Rooms Incorporated*, programmed VR Wedding Nights for Newlyweds. A clink of glasses, a slab of cake and then — OFF TO THE HOTEL WITH *Magical Mystery Rooms* — bodysheaths, fibre optics to the fingernails, to the trembling vagina and the tip of penis. And the bride and groom look just as they do in real life, floating in the stratosphere or tied to the chandelier, and when they touch it feels just the same as if he was really caressing her breast, and she strokes the virtual penis and he moans. And they love one another, oh, they love.

"Completely legit business," he said defiantly. "Come on, I received a city award for Public Health Promotion."

Bernie's sideline was less extolled although no less successful. Bernie Difiori was the creator of Hungry Night Studios, which manufactured VR erotica by the cart-load. He had an entire catalogue of preprogrammed scenarios.

"Why, just this morning I did it with Marilyn *and* JFK. We like it in the mornings, we do."

He offered her anything she wanted. Anything.

"Come on, I know you're a Stig maker but don't you at least wonder...don't you ever wonder what it would be like to, you know, do it with somebody special? A famous person? Your grade five teacher? Come on, it doesn't even have to be human, you know? We have any combination you might want. Leda and the Swan is popular. So is Catherine the Great. There's one with a teapot that sings when — "

Lily was repulsed by this man. She couldn't imagine how young couples could deal with him, have him determine their parameters, *trust* him with their deepest desires and their wedding night.

"I'm selling myself short."

"What?"

"I'm a jackass! Well, I bet you thought you *had* to choose from this batch. Hell no. A lot of this I keep in stock just for the unimaginative. But, come on, I'm in the business of fulfilling *your* dream. You tell me that *you* want. I'll program it."

"I want you to leave me alone. I want to go home."

It sounded so strange. Lily had not used such an outdated expression in years. When she said it, no picture came to mind. Her grandparents' house? Her parents' home? Beatrice's bedroom in the Hansen Block?

"Got a great one here with all five Marx Brothers. Even Gummo!"

"Do you turn every possible human phenomenon into a sexual act?"

"No. No, my dear, you, *you the customer* — "

Then he paused. "Come on, what do you think I am?"

"You don't want to hear it."

"Look, I'm trying to make a living, here. How am I gonna do that if I don't make what people want?"

"You could make TraveLOG-ONS."

She couldn't believe she was promoting those pathetic things.

"Bastards! That," his arms waved, "that, BELIEVE ME, is a closed shop!"

He paced the room rapidly and looked out the window. When he turned around a change had come over his face.

"I graduated the top of my class in visual tech. I was gonna do these...well, I was gonna make Films. Can you imagine? I mean, beautiful Films. Films with people in them. I had friends who wanted to be in them. And somebody was gonna write the stories. It was gonna be so...great."

His voice trailed off.

"So what happened?"

"What happened?" He shrugged. "I woke up. Come on, I was *dreaming*! Two hour movies, with people in them? Ordinary stories about ordinary people? They laughed me out of the corporations."

"So why didn't you start your own?"

"What do you think this is?" A sweeping motion around the room. "You're looking at it."

"*Hungry Night Studios*?"

"And *Magical Mystery Rooms, Inc.*, don't forget that. And that, my dear, is the best that I can do in this market. So, if you're bored and you want a thrill, any thrill, let me know. If not, I got work to do."

Lily had found three water-damaged books in an old desk drawer. Beatrice would love them. Pictures of all the old time movie stars, gangsters, cowboys, a demure Carole Lombard.

Earlier, Bernie had heated up some refried beans and opened a can of spaghetti. He didn't bother talking to her during their meal. He was engrossed in the particulars of his latest wedding night program. He flipped through the pages of specs. Periodically, he would snicker and shake his head.

"Make it a bit bigger, okay?" he said nervously, imitating some poor bridegroom. "Can you take the birthmark off?"

Lily moved a straight-backed chair to the window and plopped herself down. The window glass was too dirty to see through, but Lily could make out shapes and forms moving below.

Suddenly she remembered the pictures. She had been advised against carrying any but she had not been able to part with them. She pulled them out from between her two layers of socks.

Bea.

She could see Beatrice jumping hopscotch on the court behind the Lister Apartments. Head bobbing with each jump, body contorted as she bends on one leg to pick up the stone. Turning, tipping, holding, and jumping back.

— *I did it, Mama!*

Bernie was looking over Lily's shoulder at the photographs of Beatrice.

"Come on, talk to me. Give me details."

Lily couldn't believe that she was pouring her guts out to this man. He was loathsome in all the ways she cared to ponder, yet there she was telling him private moments she had shared with her daughter. And he nodded as if he understood!

"She's a Stig," Lily said deliberately.

"She looks like a nice little kid to me."

Lily had fallen asleep and when she awoke Bernie was once again in the small kitchen area of the studio. He had a pencil behind his ear.

"Always wear it when I'm working," he said. "Real operational."

He handed her her photographs of Beatrice.

"How'd you — ?" Lily grabbed them.

"I took the liberty. Come on, I just borrowed them."

"To do what?"

Then it hit her. This pervert made sleazy interactive programs. And he had Bea's face.

"You bastard! What did you do with her? You bastard!"

Bernie stepped back, clearly shaken.

"Christ, Saint Lily, self-control!"

He smoothed the front of his shirt and adjusted his pencil.

"I got something. It's not great. I don't have her exact parameters and I don't know enough detail. It's just something. If you want it."

And it was in *Magical Mystery Rooms, Inc.*, or *Hungry Night Studios*, that Lily had her virtual visit with Beatrice.

She was in the bodysheath. Her head was connected to the system. Blind. She had allowed herself to be hooked up by this man and now she was blind.

"You're gonna feel sensations all through, okay? I made it simple. Nothing weird. Now, you see the street?"

A street appeared. Trees, a curb, a sidewalk. Lily seemed to be on the sidewalk. She turned her head slightly. She could see on either side of her. Houses, a confectionery on the corner. She felt the sidewalk under her feet. When she lifted her hand, a hand appeared in front of her. She squeezed her fist and felt it. The hand closed tight.

"What do I do? Bernie? What do I do?"

"Just do what you always do. Start walking."

Lily lifted her foot. She was walking into the picture.

"Now listen, when you get to the corner don't go off to the right. I didn't get time to work it up. The immersion won't work if you go that way."

Lily stopped at the corner. She looked right and the scene tracked right.

And the world stopped! Blue and green floated shapeless within lines that looked like map coordinates. *Terra incognita.*

"Where am I?"

"Go left. Go to the house three doors down. The one with the flowers."

Lily turned away from the void, and was once more inside the world of the street. There were old-fashioned automobiles by the curb. The smell of roast beef. Someone was playing a quiet piece of music on piano. Lily heard it through the open window.

She came to the third house. A border of salvia, a few marigolds.

"Where are you?"

"The edge of the walk."

"Okay. This is where I cut out for a few minutes. I'm here if you need me, okay? I just don't want to butt in. Is the Debussy okay?"

"What? Oh, yeah, fine."

"I took a chance. Good. Well, you don't need me blabbing, here...."

"Bernie?"

"Just knock on the door."

Lily reached up. Tapped and stepped back.

The door opened. A small hand brushed hair from her eyes.

Beatrice.

"Oh...!"

The little girl held out her hand. Lily reached and felt a tactile bond. The child gripped back.

The living room was alien to her. But the chair...it was almost exactly like the chair she and Bea sat in at home.

"Can you...can I?"

Lily sat down on the hard-backed chair in the *Hungry Night*

Studios. But it wasn't the *Hungry Night Studios*, it was the dull pink brocade chair she remembered. She held out her arms.

Beatrice climbed into her lap.

Lily buried her face in Bea's hair.

No scent.

Of course. He wouldn't have had.... Lily stifled a cry and pulled Beatrice closer while Debussy played on.

The little girl turned in Lily's lap and smiled up at her mother. She did not speak. Lily rocked the child back and forth in her arms.

*

Rising from her bed and drawing back the drapery. Outside, below, the Piazza della Signoria is noisy with animals and laughter, shouting, singing.

Inside, a small cry. Smiling, reaching for the child, placing her at the breast and returning to the window.

Below, chickens are dying, bread is being sold, the man with the bubo is gone from the corner, the woman who sells the terracotta is dancing. She wheels like a top on her flat blistered heels.

Above, the morning chill still on the floor, the baby's hand across her breast. She breathes in deeply. It is raining caresses.

*

He was going to a party on the Net.

"It's a Come As You Aren't! Sure you don't want to tag along? Come on, it'll be great. I mean, you don't have to be the saint. You don't even have to be particularly nice. In fact, I'm hoping to meet up with this stellar little somebody I had the pleasure of once before. She was a flower girl at the millennium. You know, the big show; 'What If You Gave A Party and *Everyone* Came?' Well, she's all grown up now and believe me that new scent ain't roses."

Lily continued staring at the dirty translucent windows. It had been two days since she had touched her daughter's head. Her hand still tingled at the thought of it.

"Thanks, but I'd rather get hit by a truck."

"It can be arranged!" Bernie swooned.

He was wearing terrible cologne, which Lily found absurd since he was going to sit by himself in the operations room, his 'den of iniquity', plugged into a machine.

Lily watched him preen.

"At the party, I'll be in my blue-jay pelt smoking jacket."

THE PLAGUE SAINT   49

He winked at Lily, clicked his tongue, and headed down the hall.

Lily washed the dishes and stacked them on the sideboard. Her stomach was cramping, the result of too many late meals and too few encounters with vegetables.

"Well, there is Bernie," she muttered.

She wandered down the hall and stood outside the operations room. She could hear Bernie inside, smarming and laughing.

Lily went back to her cot and lay down. She smelled the leftover waft of Bernie's cologne. He was right, she thought; the real world was lonely. She touched her hand to her cheek. Yes, it had felt like that. Beatrice's hair, her fair smooth face.

Oh, Beatrice.

The experience had brought her immediate delight followed by unspeakable sadness.

Two days ago.

And, just this morning, the media flashing the face of a man who had followed the trail of the would-be saint.

"That's the creep from the belltower!"

Bernie squinted. "Ugly coot. *Why* didn't you kill him?"

Beatrice would be seeing the pictures, too. And hearing the stories. How could Anna make her understand?

"Can I get a message through at this point?"

Bernie took another swig of cough medicine, a habit that had become more apparent as the days wore on.

"My dear, everything is possible. Come on, you live in a world where everything is always, *always* possible."

He licked his lips. "Except, maybe, a decent Cherry Rumba aftertaste."

They encoded a message. Lily composed it while Bernie hid it.

"I can't send it from here, of course. Too risky. I'll run into your friend Giulia at the party. I'll let her know where it is."

"But," Lily paused, "but the party isn't real, it's in there!"

Bernie took her hand and, before she could resist, placed it on his chest.

"Am I real, Saint Lily?"

His shirt was open. The hair on his chest felt like a pot scrubber.

"In there," he nodded, "it's just as real. I have friends in there. Don't worry."

They would hide the information in 'The Picture Gallery,' a forum on the Net which contained a series of photographs that could be called up at will.

"I have a picture of my Ma in there, bless her soul. Everybody we know, everybody *friendly*, knows about 'The Picture Gallery.' It's our pony express."

Which is what gave him the rest of the idea.

"The kid likes westerns, right?"

Lily nodded.

Bernie flipped through the old movie books and found a photo of Audie Murphy on a horse.

"Poor guy couldn't act to save his life. They gave him this fantasy as payback for his soldiering. Did you know that?"

Lily frowned.

"He was, I think, America's most decorated soldier of the whole Second World War. So they let him be anything he wanted to be. And he wanted to be a movie cowboy. Wild, eh? Pure fantasy. Just like *Magical Mystery* —"

"— or *Hungry Night* —"

"— *Studios*, yup."

Bernie got busy at the terminal. Lily had no idea what he was doing. Something he called Pixel Magic.

"Your friend, Giulia, she'll know what to do. She'll find it."

The message was encoded in a virtual photograph of Audie Murphy on his horse. The photograph was now hanging in 'The Picture Gallery.'

Lily didn't know how it would work from there. Bernie said "Trust Me" in a way that made protest useless, not because he sounded particularly trustworthy, but because his voice had the finality in it that reminded her she had no other choice but this, but Bernie strutting down the hall with Cherry Rumba on his breath, with *Knock 'Em Dead* cologne seeping out of every pore.

Beatrice.

> *I feel you. I feel you close. Bet you never thought you'd find anything in his horse, eh?*

Anna:

> *Explain to her. Reassure her. Say what you have to. Take*

care of my child.

The sun drained through the window. Lily remembered Sunday afternoon, quiet sunlight, sitting on the carpet and leaning back against the armchair, daydreaming with a book in her hand as rain welled along the edges of the leaves, rimmed the flat patio bricks and framed her mother's voice humming something in the kitchen. An afternoon they would later call wasted because of the shower despite the pale sun.

She remembered a radio song on the golden oldie station. Sandy Denny's lovely voice moving through the room with such grace that even Lily's father was forced to stop and listen. No disco beat, no falsetto. Just clear tones, a voice singing "Who Knows Where the Time Goes?"

Lily smiled, mouthing the words, remembering the details of an afternoon, the rightness of the rain, stillness of the house, the tribute to the singer who had recently lost her life, the aroma of the patio herb garden, the weak but persistent sun.

Bernie had encountered Rosamunde Betty, the flower girl. This, he said, made the party complete.

"Someone mentioned all the new pictures in the Gallery," he said, which was the only reference to the information transfer.

"So it's sent?"

"People like pictures of cowboys."

Lily watched him doing his own Bernie Difiori imitation of a bandy-legged cowboy.

"Sheriff Galileo," she murmured.

With celestial half-moon perspiration stains.

He was in his own way repulsive, heading down the hall to "try out" one of the brides he was programming for *Magical Mystery*.

"Deflowering is *not* as good in there," he admitted. "But it still has that edge, you know? Come on, here's Bernie claiming King's Right four, five times a week."

But there were other times when he seemed content to sit and play a game of cards with Lily. Tea on the back burner, "rotting the pot". One afternoon during a snowstorm he covered her in a grey camp blanket and hustled her up to the roof. He opened the steel door.

They were children's flakes, the kind of snowflakes only children saw, perfect and slowly swirling.

Bernie laughed and threw his arms out and whirled in circles. He scooped up a handful of the powder and adorned the top of his head. He held out his hand to Lily.

"Saint Lily," he bowed.

The blanket around her was a robe, heavy, musty, snow-laden.

Lily put her hand up to his. They danced silently and with strange seriousness.

They stood for some time after that and Lily talked about rooftops and the telescope and Beatrice. When they went back inside Bernie hunted and found a box of emergency candles. They lit all of them; there were candles on the table, on the sideboard.

"Nice," Lily said, surveying the effort.

Candlelight played along the surfaces, the counter, the bridge of Lily's nose.

It looked like stars, or the inner chapel of a cloister.

*

It was not long after this that Bernie got into the *Rebuilt Worlds* file. Lily had not dared mention what she'd heard about the saint, Domenica da Paradiso. Perhaps she had it wrong. Perhaps it was all wrong, this rumour. She trusted Giulia and Alex, but...but she trusted no one. Anna, maybe, because she simply had to. Yet she trusted nobody but Beatrice.

Bernie had stumbled upon the files in one of his assaults on the system, as he put it. He had burrowed in while he was looking for something else. He wanted Lily to know that the Church had begun drawing up a list of witnesses for the canonization hearings. Clearly they felt that Lily's situation was well in hand.

"I don't know," he said, more to himself than to Lily. "They've been relying heavily on those *Rebuilt Worlds* files."

"In what way?"

"There's an *Institute for Rebuilt Worlds*. They compile all source information about a place or a time. Right now it's still pretty eclectic. Depends on the whims of the compiler. Rome is big. Greece. For some reason, the Depression of the 1930s."

"So...so, what's special about that? I can go and access any library book I want."

"Yes, but you have to do the cross-reference. You have to check facts. This way, it's done. Then — "

Bernie practically whispered when he said it.

"Then they rebuild them. On the Net. Virtual Rome. Like that?"

"Like Rome?"

"Virtual Rome 67 a.d.. Virtual Rome 300 a.d.. A Time Machine," he breathed. "A *Rebuilt World*. The ultimate home movie!"

Lily felt a shiver move through her.

*

The Church of the Survivors was studying Florence of the 1340s. They were interested in Florence of the 1630s.

"All plague stuff."

Lily nodded. He didn't have to say anything else. She knew, somehow, that she had to do this. There were things in there, maybe answers. If the Church was hooked into this, she had to know what they knew.

And so, the next afternoon Lily was led into the operations room. She felt, again, the fibre connect her body from head to toe. Bernie warned her about pulling out, calling out if she needed help. He made her study a map of Florence to give her some sense of direction. He warned her that the program was still under construction and that in cases where some historical fact was disputed, the image might be broken or replaced with an image from an earlier or later period. He also told her that the Mindset Monitor was not connected and she might be forced to deal with the Italian-only version of the program.

"Look at it like this. It's the way to 'Get Historical!' No wonder the Church eats it up! 'The Church of Forever Today.' Not exactly temporally inclined themselves. There," he adjusted a strap.

She was ready. She kept her eyes closed until she received the signal from Bernie.

Lily opened her eyes. And stepped into Firenze.

part 2

I am wearing someone else's shiver.

Pressing her way along the walls that lead to the *mercato*, she walks over flat Roman stones and when she looks up again the Piazza della Republica is a Roman forum, the archway now the ancient entrance to the city. Men in robes walk toward it from the Roman Baths. The light turns the archway to bronze.

Lily steps to one side and blinks and it is the *mercato* again, the bleat of lambs and the smell of chickens, piles of purple artichokes, the red tomatoes, "*Pomodori, pomodori!*", held out to her, a lemon that looks like a late summer sun. In the corner of the market, a family has set up shop, a voice importunes passersby. He holds a bottle of liquid up to his head, his face animated. He smells the elixir, smiles, and proffers it to the gentleman in the dark cloak. "*Medici,*" the man scoffs, moves along the stalls, and will have nothing to do with this hawker of oils.

The tall towers dwarf her as she moves through the square. She follows the smell of roasted meat to the stall of the chicken farmer. He does not seem to see her and keeps about his business of wringing necks. She reaches out to shield her face from the fire which flares with dripping chicken fat and in doing so touches a banner beside the stall.

And is standing in the Piazza della Republica. Yes, and the market is still there, but the chicken farmer is gone, or at least has moved over; in his place a leather-worker is displaying his wares. She begins walking. Everywhere she looks she sees the Medici *palle*, the six balls on plaques, on coats of arms decorating houses, over archways. The streets approaching the piazza are a blur of colour, ladies in long cerulean blue, in embroidered bodices; gentlemen in silks.

She passes a building in the Piazza San Giovanni. Immediately, a group of wildly-dressed men emerges, red robes, crosses, their heads hooded. They look like flamboyant Ku Klux Klan devotees. They walk with purpose across the square and disappear behind the Duomo.

She has never seen anything like it, the Duomo, Santa Maria del Fiore, crouched like a huge exquisite animal, and the tower rising by it a strand of perfection as effortless as a puff of smoke, the stones like lace-work, like an altar-cloth. To climb to the top of that tower would be to climb to the top of the world, she thinks.

It has gotten cold. She pulls the cloak around her shoulders. Out of nowhere, a winter wind. They are all moving past her now, all pushing toward the far end of the piazza to the via del Proconsolo. Lily feels herself drawn along with them; it is so easy to follow along, down the cold grey street with its tombstone-coloured buildings, toward the tall medieval tower around the bend.

"Andrea," someone shouts, *"Andrea di Domenico Passignani!"*

The tower frightens her as she watches the young man, Andrea, brought out before the crowd. His neck looks too small, too thin from where she stands, but it is fitted and he is flung and he dangles twitching before her eyes.

The crowd lets out a collective "Aaaahhh!" There is silence. And then one and then another voice begins to mutter about the Bargello and the *nibi* and goes on its way. Lily looks up at the young body swinging like a caught star outside the Bargello window. She must know what — what is happening here, she must....

"Lily. LILY!"
World skid. Stops.

*

"Sorry, Lily. You were getting pretty drawn in, there, and I know there were a few glitches. What time were you in?"

Lily's eyes focused on the operations room, on Bernie's face. She blinked twice. Bernie was still there.

"Lily?"

She tried to speak.

"Lily, come on! You were slapping around in time, there. It should be the early 1600s. Hopefully 1630. Now listen: it seems that you stay in the desired time unless you trigger a shift. Unfortunately, I don't know what the hell triggers it. But, and this is important, okay, you are not an active participant. Understand? The program allows for some interaction but we don't really know the parameters or coordinates so it would be better for you to just mostly look, okay? Like in the gift shop? *Lovely To Look At, Delightful To Hold, But If You Drop It, Consider It Sold?* Things get too complicated otherwise. Oh, and your visage is consistent."

Lily stared.

"I mean, you look the way they do. Your clothes, like that. Okay? Pay attention! Listen, this is plague time, here, and we're looking at a city that knows a lot about the plague. By all means, walk around. Listen to people. As much as you can, anyway. Looks like the Mindset Monitor screws up the translation. Something screwy. They should have come to *Hungry Night* for that. So, listen, unless *you* know Renaissance Italian, be a good little tourist and don't go shooting your mouth off, okay?"

Bernie's lower lip was twitching. Whiskers were growing on his face, she could see them growing as he spoke. A white hair pushed through a follicle on his head and laid itself like translucent fishing line along the water.

"I just watched them execute a man. Andrea de Domenico Passignani," she said.

Lily found herself remembering one Easter, the Easter of the chickens. Her friend Marie-Ange had hunted for her Easter eggs just as Lily had, but while Lily had found the usual assortment of Mr. Big Buns and Peter Rabbits, Marie-Ange had found a small blue live chick. They had been very popular that year and the children had been delighted as only children could be when faced with absolute control over something. They converted a shoe box into a home and with the approval of both sets of parents set up watch on the 'nursery.' A small clock ticked in the corner of the box, something that forever after bothered Lily. It was supposed to be mother, to be like a mother to the painted blue bird that seemed to cheep all the time. They fed it and watered it. There was a light to keep it warm.

Easter came and went but the girls were vigilant. The bird lived in Marie-Ange's basement but Lily took her turn watching it after school and on weekends. They named it, of course. Its name was Stella Robitaille. Lily and Mary-Ange had both liked Stella. Robitaille was Marie-Ange's last name.

They took good care. They took such good care that the bird grew, and lost most of its dye, and turned into a rather temperamental blue-white chicken. It lived, then, in an old television that had had the picture tube removed. Stella Robitaille strutted through endless hours of television to the initial delight and then unease of Marie-Ange and Lily.

They loved Stella, who smelled, who nipped them. They had plans to free her on a farm in the country. Marie-Ange's parents always went to the country twice a year to visit relatives. The girls sat planning Stella's future, a future that played across the blank television screen in the basement.

The end of Stella's life came suddenly. A brief pain, Marie-Ange's mother said, or maybe even no pain, who knew what chickens felt? The cruelty of serving the chicken to Marie-Ange was never surpassed. The child bolted and ran, and Lily ran the other way.

"What a world," Lily's father had said, handing her a rubber stamp that proclaimed, *What a World!*
They buried the clock in the shoe box.
Lily dreamed of the underground clock for many years.

"HELLO, LILY!"
Bernie's five-o'clock shadow in her face.
"Stick with me here, okay?"
She felt dizzy. She wanted to see Beatrice, to take her daughter and get on a train to another country, like in the old war movies, get on in one country and get off in the Alps, everybody meeting on that pathway over the Alps, refugees, the family from *The Sound of Music*, Lily and Beatrice finding a new life eating goat cheese and drinking the milk of Charolais cows.

She wanted her *Snoopy* pen and her *Barbie* lunch-box, the half-moon cakes her mother packed inside, the tollhouse cookies her mother sliced and baked right from the tube. She wanted that nylon squall jacket that disappeared when she was ten, just vanished off the face of the earth, bewildering her for weeks. She wanted the marbles in the blue cloth bag, the perfect cats' eyes, the smokies, the beauties, the large Bullies everybody else called Shooters.

Stupid things to cry for.

The boy hanging from the window like a star.

"Okay Lily, stop, okay? Come on, we'll access it, okay? Tell me his name again?"
Lily's head was throbbing.
Bernie called up a file. "There...see? Right there. The guy died for breaking into a sealed house, see? 'White Cross on the Door.' A plague-infested house."

Bernie's voice lost its edge.

"He died for stealing from a house they'd sealed."

It was that simple. And it would be that simple again. "His confession was extracted under torture," Bernie added.

"What did he steal?" Lily heard herself ask.

"I don't know. Here, a cloak. And a *celone*, uh, it says like a tablecloth or something."

Lily shook her head. "Listen, could you make sure I don't have to witness that again?"

Bernie said they were still fine-tuning.

*

She is down by the Arno. It is hazy and almost unbearably humid. The Arno is a pretty sewer; she remembers Bernie saying that. Bodies, wool dye, everything goes into the Fiume d'Arno. Savonarola's ashes, the bodies of the executed, the murdered, the bad meat, the bad fruit, all flung into the crowded waters.

From where she is standing Lily can see a woman chasing pigeons by the water. Her raw legs are visible beneath the layered skirt. She waddles under her own weight, swearing in a rhythm that is vaguely operatic.

She catches the bird and it scrambles, flaps and scuttles, baring non-existent teeth. She takes her knife to it cleanly and slits it, nearly quarters it. Then she lifts her skirt. A horrible mess. Against the matted hair, a blue swelling as big as a cantaloupe, a festering scab the size of a fist. The woman swoons, suddenly appearing to dance with the dripping feathers, then she places the opened bird across the *bubo* and throws her head back in rattling prayers.

Oh yes, Lily knows they are prayers.

The woman prays to the Madonna, to the patron saints and protectors of the city. It even seems as though she is praying to the pigeon. A grotesque choreography. Props that don't work. Lily remembers her father's face as he watched her mother behind the glass. The gurgle that couldn't seem to leave his throat, the saliva and the prayers.

The woman sees her, shrieks, and tosses the pigeon into the river. Her skirt falls around her and she curses the air between herself and Lily. She moves like a shoplifter with a turkey between her legs. Lily wants to laugh at the horror. To call out.

Her voice catches in her throat.

The summer Lily and her three desperate girlfriends decided to become security guards. Sitting in an airless office above the retail floor, watching a film about people who take things.

"Who steal," the asthmatic trainer had said, but it actually sounded worse when he wheezed, "people who take", as they witnessed actual films of women putting on the third skirt in the dressing room, of men shoving bar equipment into pockets, corkscrews and shot glasses down their pants. The turkey was one of the truly inspired, truly reckless acts. Lily sat open-mouthed as the bird was hoisted beneath the skirt, clamped with the force of the woman's thighs, Lily supposed. A frozen turkey. Lily had thought that the woman deserved to keep it. Like the man with the roast beef on his head, hidden under a wool toque in summer. Blood dripping down his temples.

Things.

Lily is down by the water now. Along comes a young girl. She may be eight or nine. She is small, very capable, as she moves along the bank. She sees Lily and smiles. Her dress is dusty brown, like the stones.

"Mama," she says.

And then "Mama, Mama," a slow deliberate chant.

The woman with the *bubo*.

Lily steps toward the child, who starts.

"Mama!"

Lily points further down along the river.

"Mama," she says softly.

The girl looks at the river, then back at Lily, and pushes away.

Lily watches her picking her way among the weeds. In Lily's own childhood it would be bottles and tires, the cardboard boxes of the homeless.

While she has been watching the girl, she is aware that a boy is fishing on the far bank. The fly is cast and lands so lightly on the surface that the entire act is a pantomime of itself. Lily marvels at the boy. He is impervious. Lily feels that she could watch him forever, that she has been watching him forever. Something in the snap of the wrist which, even at this distance, is both economical and extravagant. The sun sears the water. Surely it is not a good time to be fishing. And what might he catch.... The boy retrieves his line and casts again religiously. Wildflowers along the bank. He is engulfed, from here, in a mass of yellow flowers. Lily smiles.

It is later and the sun is kinder now, gilding the river and the Ponte Vecchio. The boy has gone, running up the bank with something dangling from the line in his outstretched hand.

She wishes she had that map he'd shown her, though she was never good at reading maps. Seemed little need for the skill when you never went anywhere. And yet there was a mania for them. In the offices Lily cleaned there were maps on all the walls, maps of the New World, maps of outer space, tiny stagecoaches patterning the map of the Old West. Charts of sea voyages, the spawning routes of east coast salmon. Beatrice's star charts all over her bedroom wall. Lily never realized before how strange that was.

Don't get lost. Bernie's advice.

"Don't get lost, Lily," her mother calling out as Lily wrestled with her kite. It had climbed alright but was now too close to the box kite; the strings were dangerously close.

"You hear me?"

Lost! Lily looked over incredulously. All her mother had to do was look for the kid with the knotted kite string, the kid hanging on for dear life. Geez!

Lily remembers some of the names from Bernie's map. She hears the bells of Santa Croce and follows them, pausing at the via de'Neri. She steps into the street and the image grids and suddenly she is further back, the dress medieval. She hides in a doorway as the procession passes, two bound men, accompanied by a small group of people.

A woman emptying her apron crumbs on the street stiffens, crosses herself, and shoves her child indoors. *"Compagnia dei Neri,"* the woman breathes. The first prisoner looks at her. Then he turns to Lily, and Lily knows that she is looking at someone who is about to die.

She can't stay here. Lily waits until they have passed and then retraces her steps to the point where she crossed into the street. She steps back from it and the image disappears. She is relieved to see the brighter clothes, the graceful Renaissance arches.

What is she looking for? How is she supposed to know? She is in the Piazza Santa Croce. The church. It is huge. Even for now, that is, for her time, it would be huge. Images of St. Francis everywhere. His life, his death. Giotto, Lily remembers, from an art course ages ago. Whenever. The dark light of the church. Giotto's Francis. The walls flicker. At first Lily thinks it is the candlelight. Tombs appear along the walls. She stands before Michelangelo's tomb. Sad figures reflecting. She continues walking, and genuflects in front of the altar.

It is when she is on the left side of the church that it happens. She has been trying to get a feel for the immensity of the building and she leans back against the wall. There is a strange sensation and she turns and gasps.

Another tomb has appeared directly behind her.

Galileo.

Galileo peering up to the heavens. Lily remembers. But isn't he still alive? Isn't he about to stand trial right about —

She steps back from the tomb, which glows brightly and disappears. This corner of the church goes dark.

Not yet.

Oh, Bea. Galileo.

They are beginning a service. Lily recedes further into the shadows and listens to the rising and falling voices. Her grandfather had liked Gregorian chants; Lily listened to some as a child. They echo through the basilica, up to the painted wooden beams.

Lily wants to pray for something. She prays for Beatrice as she always does, a combination of a daydream and a memory, a picture of Beatrice, the light along her face, her voice reciting a little rhyme deep into the night. Are these prayers? Lily breathes and hears her breath somewhere in the wave of voices.

Big change is scary.

A total stranger said that to her on the eve of the millennium. He seemed totally preoccupied with where he was standing as they all waited through the countdown, shifting a few inches to the left, then back. He was lining himself up under some star. He wanted to be in the right place at the right time. And suddenly as the countdown from ten began, he turned to Lily and said, "Big change is scary."

Lily lost count.

A thousand years were gone in a second.

The chanting continued and Lily chanted as well, silently, backwards from ten.

Outside in the piazza again, Lily sits, exhausted. She wants to sleep but there is something wrong with the idea. If she falls asleep here, where will she wake up? A boy rolls a ball over the stones. She would like to see what the ball is made of but she is too tired to move.

How do you get out of here?

It's not like she can step back through the looking glass. It's not like she can tug on her line like an underwater diver.

I want to come up.

Lily rests her face in her hands.

And hears the horse snort. Looks up just in time to see it charging in her direction. She throws herself over and the horse thunders past. The rider reins in the horse. Lily's eyes widen. The rider is Lorenzo the Magnificent; she remembers the poster from art class. He turns and the jousting tournament continues. Lily pulls herself up from the stones. The image flashes and disappears.

Swallows circle the church. An old man with urine-drenched trousers is singing to himself as he shuffles past. The birds join in the chorus. Lily nurses her shoulder. And everything goes black.

She doesn't know how much time has passed, maybe a minute, perhaps an hour. It was like the "bad trips" her Uncle Philly used to tell her about, where you couldn't wake up from the dream.

"Coming down, honey, that was hard."

Lily has expected to see...she opens her eyes and hopes she'll see Beatrice, her quilted robe, her face animated as the cowboy dusts off his stetson.

"Mama, is that Jeff Chandler?"

Lily looking at the screen and replying, "Randolph Scott."

Instead, she watches as a beggar makes his rounds in the piazza. She can't stay here. She picks herself up.

Wandering, Lily, you are wandering. You're lost, dark alley after dark alley, did you pass this way before? Where did Bernie say? What is there to avoid?

"That's just it," her Uncle Philly's voice. "You're right there, man, and everything is heightened, like real versions of themselves, you know? Fuck Plato's cave, man, it's, like, the real thing!"

Lily on the dark narrow road, hears the gnawing, kicking.

Shudders.

They smell her. They roar.

Lily covers her ears and runs the gauntlet of sound. The Roman lions. The amphitheatre lions. And Lily a saint? A martyr?

She hears them until she reaches the corner. As she crosses the intersection the roaring stops, the echoes fade.

Silence.

There ought to be little signs, she shivers, hearing Uncle Philly's laughter in the background.

She knows she could not do it. Not like that, not tossed into the ring with a starved animal. Every church here boasted paintings of their saints, the flesh peeling, the limbs broken. The saint with the pincers, the saint on the wheel, the saint with her severed breasts in a bowl.

The Church of the Survivors is looking for a plague saint, combing the defunct diners of Medicine Hat, hovering in the derelict towers of Toronto, in shadows of the ghost towns of the east. They are looking for a saint to carry all their burdens right up to the stratosphere, the ionosphere, to take their parcel of woes to the constellations themselves, to the double stars of Theta Orionis, of Alpha Centauri, star clusters brimming with human tears. The anonymous words from so long ago, a song of the long-dead:

The small stars are trembling
Orion and the Pleiades.

Lily remembers. Remembers that she remembers.

It is only when he is pulling on her arm that she realizes he has been calling out to her all along. A youngish man with black curls, with a haggard face for one his age. Only how does she know how old these people are? She had been watching his face unaware that he has been seeking out hers. He is short of breath. He talks brokenly and rapidly.

Per favore...prego —"

He puts his arm around Lily's shoulder.

"Ambasci...mal di petto. Presto!"

She is being pulled down the via — "Where are we going? Hey!"

The man looks at her strangely.

"Prego?"

His eyes are desperate.

Lily follows him along the cobbled street, trying to note the twists and turns the road takes.

"Where.... *Dove?"* She remembers one of a couple of dozen Italian words she ever knew.

He flings his arms in exasperation. *"Piazza del Limbo!"*

A house, a dark hovel, down the alley off from the piazza. She enters behind him, instinctively ducking her head at the door frame. Smells. Close, clotted air, and sickness.

Oh, Jesus.

She can't be more than seven. Lily can barely make out the rest of the room. The candles are beside the child, who is contorted on a small bed. She has been gasping for breath and has remained this way. Two older girls and a young boy are watching from the shadows. They are all staring at Lily. So is the man. What is she supposed to do?

Lily approaches the cot, reaches out her hand...God...touches the forehead.

The child is burning.

She is beyond movement. Lily pulls back the stinking blanket, filthy bedclothes.

"Off! Take these off!"

Lily points to the nightshirt.

"Get me another one... Clean."

They follow her hands and eyes. They are praying aloud now, as they seem to believe she is. The oldest girl brings Lily things at random.

"No. Don't you have any — ?"

Finally a little shirt.

"Good! I need water and a cloth. Water...*aqua...agua.*" Lily makes drinking motions with an invisible cup.

The child's mouth opens slightly; she takes shallow breaths, too infrequently. The older girl returns with a cloth and a terracotta bowl filled with water.

"Terrific," Lily nods. She begins sponging water across the forehead, the drops dampening the girl's temples and sliding into her dark frizzy hair. Lily washes and pats the little body. She has never felt this helpless. She can't even offer useless words of comfort. She wants to cry. She wants Beatrice. She wishes she could remember a prayer, any prayer.

Now I lay me down to sleep

What did she used to say?

Angel of God, my guardian dear,
To whom God's love entrusts me here,
Ever this day be at my side
To light and guard, to rule and guide.
Amen.

She has been whispering. When she reaches the *Amen* she glances up from the child. The other children and the father are kneeling, heads bowed. When she reaches the *Amen*, they say *Amen*.

The thin boy stands before her. He has a scab on his lip. He has tears in his eyes.

"Anjelica," he strokes his little sister's hand. And to Lily, imploringly, "Anjelica."

The candle is low. The children are asleep on a bench in the corner. The father has fallen asleep on a chair beside the bed. Lily has been examining the child's dainty hand and thinking of her nights with Beatrice. Her teething and the early fevers. That was a time Lily had felt particularly alone. It was at times like that that she wished there had been a husband, a partner to watch over Beatrice, someone to play cards with through the night as they took turns changing diapers and fussing with fever medication. Edward would have done that if he had had the chance. He would have calmed his daughter.

Lily looks over at this young man. How did his life turn out like this? How old is he? Where is his wife in the middle of this crisis? He has a tired face, but who wouldn't? His face is also kind. A sharply defined jaw. A strong nose. He would be considered a model in her day. He would drive a small Italian sports-car, pose for designer ads, star in TraveLOG-ONS depicting ski chalets and crackling fires.

She feels the forehead again. A cool stillness.

The fever!

"Oh...."

She checks the head again, leans over and feels the face, the neck and the chest.

"Senore," she nudges the father.

He opens his eyes.

Lily points to his child. "The fever. Gone!" She makes a Poof! sign, a magician's pass, with her hand.

The man puts his lips to the child's forehead. Turns. Takes Lily's hand in his and holds it, his head lowered. Lily feels his hair against her arm, reaches down and rests her hand on his head. He has taken her for someone else, mistaken her for a healer. Lily shakes her head and backs away.

"Just lucky," she gesticulates.

The man hears the foreign words, probably thinks she is speaking in tongues, probably thinks she can take the smell from the destitute wildflowers rotting in the small clay pot.

The older daughter will sit with the children. He wants Lily to follow him. Lily emerges from the stunted doorway into the alley. A church bell is tolling. They make their way back to the piazza.

"Piazza del — ?"

The man is again puzzled by her question.

"Piazza del Limbo."

Lily remembers. The place where they used to bury the unbaptized babies.

They approach the small medieval church. The portal looks newer than the rest of the front. Like the renovations to the mini-malls, except this renovation is Renaissance. People are filing in around them. The man is hesitating. Lily doesn't know why they have come here but she is not about to stand blocking a doorway so she threads her way in with the rest of the parishioners. The man follows behind her but as she takes a seat near the back he passes her and walks toward the altar.

Candles. A few flowers. A simple coffin for a simple funeral. She sees the man bow his head. The man brushes his hand along the coffin. It is the same goodbye Lily's father stroked onto the window separating himself and his dead wife.

The man's grief is reflected in the faces of the faithful. The bell stops tolling. A service begins. The flowers in the clay pot could have been for the woman, or could have been picked by her one recent afternoon down by the river, her daughters and son in tow, the older daughter walking along ahead, the man smiling at this family from the bridge, on his way to work. Lily's father stamping *Catch You Later!* on her hand before heading out the door, her mother whipping up a yogurt shake for breakfast. The disco beat and the blur of the blender and outside, maybe, birds.

Lily tries to understand what they are saying.

"Ginevra." Your servant Ginevra, she was...Lily can't quite make out...thirty...thirty-four? Ginevra, Lord, your servant, *Dio, Dio*, thank you for having blessed the marriage, for the children, for the boy who will work in the shop and the girls who will care for the house and for their father, *Matteo.*

Matteo.
Matteo is slumped beside the coffin. Matteo is thanking God?

She was the afternoon light on the Arno.
She was the white flowers growing in the hills.
She was clean, oh Lord, she did not die of the *pistolenza.*
Dio, Dio, per piacere, put her into consecrated ground.

The bell begins again. The procession is unbearably slow. Matteo is behind his wife, leaving the church with her this one last time, this church in which they were married, in which their children were baptized. The sunlight in the piazza seems excessive, abundant. The sudden freshness of the air is intoxicating. Lily breathes deeply. Closes her eyes. When she opens them the people beside her seem to be watching her for signs. She lifts her hand to her head and tries to take off the gear. Then she looks down at her hands. Her hands seem so old.

I want to come out.

Lily sent to her room, her mother's important office documents stamped all over with offerings from her father's display box.

Get a Life!
Jim Henson Pulls Strings to Get a Job!
Visit Ann Arbor

Please, Bernie. Please.
I want to come out.

*

The operations room. A waiting room in a deserted office building. Bernie's stubbled face as he walked her back to the kitchen. A bar of light above their heads. Bernie making tea.

They were always looking for the easy way out. Lily remembered that from her past. The recessions, the depressions, species bowing down and bowing out, 'if a rainforest falls in the woods, does it make a sound', the exit pleas of the changing landscape. And it was always the quick fix, the least inspired, bloodshot eyes tired of victors everywhere now blinking the world into victims, into things that could be fixed.

Only they hadn't. And some things weren't fixable. And it took the better eye to tell the difference.

She couldn't talk to him. It was useless. He proffered the macaroni and she nodded. And, drying dishes later, she shifted away every time he added something to the rack.

It was late when they finished, or so it seemed, no light coming in the filthy window. Lily wrapped the grey blanket around her shoulders and sat cross-legged on the cot. Above her, old wood, probably rotting, a slab of concrete, maybe, or some bricks. A sprinkling of asbestos to make it interesting, a layer of leaded paint from the heady building years.

And the stars.
Galileo in marble on a tomb in Florence.
And the stars.
Galileo's finger a display in a museum.
And the stars.

Lily stood under the shower and let the water melt her face down. Who was she underneath, what face did the young man, Matteo, believe he saw? The smooth marble faces in the fire-dappled sacristy, the faces of her family crowded round her Christmas memory. Soft cheeks of Donatello's *David*, youth forever flourishing.

The models, all of them, were dust. Matteo was dust, if he ever

THE PLAGUE SAINT   71

existed at all. Stuck inside, forever trying to rescue his little girl, to hold her back from the great atom flow, *per favore*, keep these atoms together a little longer. I have need of them. I love this configuration, these brain patterns. I love this slightly unaligned smile and the two front teeth that are just now coming in. I love the slender arms that make their giant sweeping motions when she dances. *Per piacere, Dio, Dio*, let my *bambina* stay with me.

O, mysterium.
O, Dio.

In the morning, Bernie made an omelette with what he called arm and leg eggs. Lily had not seen fresh eggs since...she couldn't remember. She ate hungrily, forgetting salt, dragging her fork across the plate.

"C'mon, could you leave the pattern? It's part of a set!"

Bernie's coffee was atrocious, as usual. The toast was better. He hefted over a huge vat of jelly. "Can you believe, they're practically *giving* this stuff away!"

"So," he ventured again, "you really don't want to talk about it, eh?"

"Please!" Lily held up her hand.

Funny gesture. She suddenly had the sensation of sitting with a hand raised in a kind of bizarre benediction, toast crumbs on the end of her fingers.

"You want to play some cards?"

He cleared the table and broke open a deck and started the nervous shuffling. It reminded Lily of that old, old movie with Shirley Maclaine...Jack Lemmon...*The Apart-ment*, Jack fidgeting through a game of gin as Shirley recovered from an overdose. Bernie was a lot like the Jack Lemmon character. Underneath the dumb-ass comments and the wisecracks was somebody who....

Bernie rattled off a set of rules.

Somebody who made pasta with a tennis racket.

"Whoo, whoo, whooooo! You *sure* you want to put down that card?"

And Shirley was the Shirley before she became New Age Shirley with the multiple pasts.

"Come to Mama, eat your heart out, smell the coffee, Baby...."

Lily concentrated on the knave of hearts.

He stole the tarts.

He took them clean away.

"...GIN!"

One thought jarred.

The Apartment was a love story.

When she was in that place it was so immediate; it was all there was. There were her memories, of course. Beatrice. But they could be muted, played upon, cast in bronze and then melted down and re-cast.

It was like love, the wholeness of it, the knowledge of being swallowed up whole in a new reality that was neither you nor the other. And it didn't have to make sense. Lily walking among the long-dead in 1630 Italy. Lily in love with an entire other human being.

She tried to remember.

She had loved like that once, when the day itself was transformed because he existed, an aluminum can in a ditch was full again, the lilac branch the kid ripped from the bush was reattached, or perhaps continued to thrive in the fist of the child on the pathway.

When there were same-day glories.

"It's full-immersion VR, this Florence thing," Bernie beamed.

Love.

And when you stepped out of it, or were thrown out, or you went to the store to buy milk and kept on going, you took off the gear, unpeeled the garments of attachment. You cleared your head.

And the world so whole, so entire, is gone.

There are tea-stains on the counter.

The windows need cleaning.

He exists somewhere but you can't get there anymore. And so, in memory, he is cast and re-cast, sometimes into a useful urn you can keep his ashes in, sometimes into an exquisite door knocker on the entrance to a *palazzo*.

Into something with all the dross thrown off.

You dust crevices in all the corners.

You pray to the Madonna of Same-Day Glories.

You are humbled. And reminded.

Love.

Bernie's father used to survey land when Bernie was a kid. Then he drove trucks for a company back east. He insisted that Bernie get an education and helped to pay for the first years of film studies despite his disappointment at the choice. After he died, Bernie's mother spiralled into a series of sad relationships, not passively stemming loneliness, but actively pursuing, attempting to recapture, the huge love she had known.

Parts of me are dead, she kept saying, when Bernie would rescue her from a bar in the afternoon. Parts of me are just falling off as if I have leprosy. Holding out her arm as though the hand was already gone.

It's okay, Mama, come on, let's go home now. C'mon, Mama.

Holding out a hand to clasp her non-existent fingers.

Lily had agreed with Bernie that his mother had not dealt with pain very well. Lily's father stamping *Deal With It!* on letters to his creditors.

But nobody loved that big anymore. And it wasn't just the Disease. People had trouble believing anymore. And if they did believe, it was in the transitory groupings of people, like fruit in a bowl, for a single blurred snapshot. Afterward, things were shifted, shoved around — throw the banana out, hide the bruises on that pear.

Nobody believed anything would last.

And they were probably right. Only the scratch of the quill saved Shakespeare's dark lady, a whisper on a corner Dante's first glimpse of Beatrice. And it was always like this. Love and its human tag-along, an old woman putting roses on a plot of earth in a field, crying, I am in love with him. Don't you see? I am in love with dust. Matteo burying his young wife as his daughter breathes faintly a half a street away. Matteo had believed. And Matteo had loved.

Bernie said he had bothered loving only twice, and each time it had ended in disaster. He did not even try for the casual bingo partner now, he said, preferring a guaranteed response in the programmable universe.

"In there, I get what I want."

Was that why people used to fall in love? To get what they wanted? Too crass, too simple.

What they needed, then?

Lily didn't understand. They went inside love because they were lonely, just like Bernie was when he brushed and gargled before heading down the hall to the equipment. They fell in love because the reaching out was like photosynthesis, or a good cup of coffee. It made you feel that the atom swarm you lived in was your own, right down to the clump of it that made up your hand. It made you feel like you could be here forever, and could belong to this forever, you, giddy, spilling sand from hand to hand.

Lily was surprised to see herself reach across the table and take Bernie's jelly-stained hand into her own.

Lily thought about Beatrice all afternoon. By evening she was once again ready to enter Firenze. She made Bernie promise it would be from another location this time. She did not want to see Matteo and the children again. Where were the canonization hearings? Where were Domenica's bones? Where was the body of the Plague Saint?

Lily nodded a goodbye to Bernie and closed her eyes.

*

The morning sun warms the pink marble of the Duomo, brings out the fine lines in the green, the cold stone smelling of urine and incense. The doors to the Baptistry blaze before her. Ghiberti's Doors. The Gates of Paradise.

Lily approaches the illuminated portal. She wants to trace her finger along the line of Eve's thigh as she emerges from nothingness into creation, but the sunlight is already doing that, as it is also warming the backs of the sheep in another panel.

Beatrice would love this, Lily thinks, surprised at how simple an observation it is. Michelangelo thought they were The Gates of Paradise. Lily Dalriada thinks her daughter might like them. Tiny sculpted heads emerge three-dimensionally from the bronze. Ghiberti, surely, one of them. Yes. The head of a man who gave his life, almost thirty years of his life, to these burnished doors.

To the Baptistry. Once, a baby named Dante cried and suckled within these walls as he was welcomed into the world, into the church. Perhaps the sun was generous on that morning long before the Doors existed.

Magnificent, Lily thinks. She has missed things of beauty. She steps back to take one final look at the doors and sees out of the corner of her eye the crucifix-emblazoned robes, the hoods. There they are again. The *Miseracordia*. Invisible, anonymous. They have heard of another plague case, perhaps, or another death. They will carry the victim to the plague hospital, or to the grave. They move across the Piazza del Duomo without feet, it seems, striding without legs, the robes swaying in a sudden morning gust as they disappear down a side street.

Like they are in a play, Lily thinks. Or like the half-time shows during the football games her grandpa made her watch. Lily fascinated by the glittery pom-poms, the steps enacted in unison. A human pyramid, an acrobatic dive from the top, a flash of batons from the sidelines, and they are gone.

Lily stands and looks to the top of Giotto's tower. Shivers. How could he have envisioned such a thing? In Lily's dreams there were no towers, and what buildings there were were modelled after the Lister Apartments, the Hansen Blocks. Only rarely did she remember the rooms of her childhood. Yet this man closed his eyes and the world became pink and green and white, a field of flowers so delicate, so perfectly delicate that they blew this way and that in the breeze. As this tower could, Lily believes. Unlike the bronze solidity of the doors which marked the boundary between earth and heaven, this tower of light and flowers could lift and float away at any time, up and over the astonished heads. Over, even, the dome.

Lily smiles, and believes. And this, she realizes, is good. To stand on a crisp sunny morning with the smell of wet stone all around you, with swallows and pigeons fluttering like a ticker-tape parade, old *padrones* out in twos strolling around the cathedral.

She remembers a children's story she'd once read about a little boy who lived in a painting. A background boy, not one of the principal figures, so insignificant that his body was not even fully realized.

He decided to escape his confines and hopped down from the painting and started wandering through the museum. He went from picture to picture always looking for the perfect place to live. He ended up in one, a background boy again, but in a painting in which he was somehow happier. Lily remembered that each picture had been its own unique world. Each was self-contained and self-absorbed, separate and complete.

She misses Beatrice. What would she be doing? Had Anna been seeing to her lessons? Had Anna taken her to the country?

Oh, Bea.

Galileo is here. I mean, was here. Is he up before the Inquisition? Sheriff Galileo. This town ain't big enough for the both of us. Yer universe throbs to its own rhythm, and ahm'a askin' you politely, here, to pack it up an' be out of town on the next stage.

Or what?

Well, let's just say, I won't be responsible for the actions of m'boys.

Beatrice. Tell Anna that wherever you are she should take you up to the roof. Is the telescope still with you? Can you see the winter constellations?

"When You Wish Upon a Star", Beatrice.

And Lily remembers. That was from *Pinocchio*. Pinocchio was from here.

Too strange.

In the market a couple of children are juggling. They are quite good; they pass fruit and then bowling pins back and forth to one another. Lily looks again. They are not children; they are dwarves, and the bowling pins are cooked joints of meat which they try to take bites from as the chunks fly past.

People clap hands and are laughing and stamping their feet. A small boy balances on his toes, reaching overhead to his mother's hands. And in the background, out in the street that rings the piazza, members of the *Miseracordia* float by with a body on their litter.

A disfigured old woman hobbles over the stones, moaning loudly, cursing the sky. Three children, arms linked, rush up to the pigeons. The image undulates like water in the basin of a moving train. She is dizzy. If she could just sit down somewhere. Over there in the corner the leather worker has set up his wares. She almost swoons at the smell of the hides. It catches in her nose, the animal, the tanning, the dyes. She can't explain; it is like she can see the animal already adorned, cows on the hill-side, their skins stamped with the gold-trimmed Medici *palle*, the Florentine fleur-de-lis across their broad foreheads.

His hands are extensions of the leather. Dark skin that is think and buttery soft and rubbed until it glows. He has grey eyes, unusual here. Eyes of a wolf, careful. He stares at Lily openly, his embossing tool falling from his hand.

"*Salvina?*"

Lily returns his stare. Who is he looking for in her eyes?

"*O, Salvina!*" He embraces Lily. His eyes as he takes her face in his hands, his lips upon hers printing a pattern, tongue like fire in her mouth. Salt-sweaty skin, his skin, stubble, eyes searching for her in the forest.

"*Salvina, Salvina.*"

Lily closes her eyes and is Salvina among the trees, her ivory linen dress open, her legs unsteady after such insistent love, rising to clasp his outstretched arm. She hears a cathedral bell tolling in a piazza somewhere nearby. She smells the leather on his fingers. She wants this. Lily. Wants this passion.

From the hill she looks down upon the red-roofed city. It is so small, so complete, like the glass domes you shook at Christmas. A small and perfect world.

They have come here before, Salvina and this man. Someone called out to *Taddeo* as they left the market.

Taddeo.

He holds her hand as they climb. Lily smells the grass. The air so thick and sultry. In the clearing behind the trees, she is not surprised when he unties the bodice of her dress; she watches the dress fall to her feet. Her shift is removed. She is bathed in the warm summer air, her skin browner than she remembers.

He stands naked before her. His body is like those of Michelangelo's burly slaves emerging from stone, thighs ripping through rock, stomachs that have withstood the press of marble for centuries.

He has been waiting for centuries. He takes her down on the soft grass and his hands and tongue are everywhere, rubbing her like leather, the smooth repetitions on her nipples, across her stomach. She feels herself clenching, opens her eyes and sees her legs unfurl like wings.

It is real. It cannot be. Does it matter? He is all the men she has never been allowed, all the men that have been forbidden women through the years. He must know this, nuzzling the inside of her thigh. If only she would walk around like this all the time, face serene, body rupturing delight, connected — Connected. She feels like a lightning rod. The electricity is going to kill her.

Christ.

Oh, she, oh, she sees them.

Fra'Angelico's wings.

He is asleep by her side. She does not tire of observing his body. The cleft of his buttock, the jut of his arching thigh. She has enjoyed Salvina's lover and is envious of a woman who can have this.

She must leave before he wakes up and wants to speak to her. Lily dresses quickly and slips on her sandals. She takes the footpath down from the hills, pausing as the bells from the cathedrals all toll the hour for vespers. Later tonight Taddeo will awaken with the moon on his back, the Pleiades tattooed between his shoulder blades.

What is she doing? This is not like her. But she knows that for the first time in a long time she feels the earth buzz beneath her as she walks shakily across the Ponte Alle Grascia back to the centre of the city.

The ladies dress beautifully here. And the men. So different from Dante's time, all hooded figures in drab cloaks, sorry for their good fortune. Here, beauty is celebrated, even flaunted. And from what she can tell it is only sometimes for the glory of God. There is an edge to it. She can't call it crass, since the merest iron doorstop is amazing. But, within the context, within *this* world, Lily questions whether beauty was ever cheapened by its abundance or its ease.

It seems there is a church on every corner. Whole lives given to a small parish in a lane. Whole lives lived anonymously in the shadow of the brilliant cathedral. She had read once that there was a disease people sometimes got when in Florence. She can't remember the name they used, but the disease itself was the 'overdose of beauty'. The heart, the eyes, overwhelmed, the body fainting before perfect forms, perfect lines. The fluid lines of Michelangelo. Walking around with that shape in your head. A curve you can't get out of your mind, and then you see it again, horrified, in the opened intestines of a dying soldier. The dusty pink on Fra' Angelico's angel cursing the fevered face of a doomed child. The stars of Fra' Bartolomeo's "Madonna con Stella" in the rainwater pooling around stones in the piazza. The sudden burden of seeing.

Lily knows that she has lived small. The Church of the

Survivors...no, no even before all that. She can't blame them for the lack of dreams in the heads on pillows back in 1980. She can't explain the cardboard box houses, the insane and sick wandering the streets, the shop owners dying for thirty-five dollars and change. Lily has lived small among these citizens, cleaning offices in the evening, house sitting for the rich. And never really looking too closely as she dusts and polishes.

The street of the coffin makers, via Ricasoli. And a lone voice intoning the *Te Deum*. A little boy daydreaming, dragging a stick along the stone walls, tap-tapping at each doorway that he passes.

Once, when people travelled, they strapped themselves into seats and left the earth. They flew in the direction of the stars. No one thought it strange to point to a night sky and declare that the next morning you would be up there, far beyond the broken dishwasher and the bent snow shovel.

If Lily had been able to travel she would have flown here, hours into the future. Hours less of her life. Hours less time with Beatrice. And she would look out at the constellations over the ocean and know that they were the same constellations that guided the ancient sailors, that still guided what sailors existed. And how would she have explained to Beatrice that as she moved over the water time was moving too, sunrises were coming one after another like apples on the good side of the tree, a little pinker, a little fuller, and in their own time.

Walking the early evening streets with warm gold on the stones, she is filled with such a seeping sultry peace that she feels, at last, that this place exists, that she exists here and now, with love still warm inside her, fingerprints still on her skin. Her feet pressing these stones lightly, leather on stone.

Breathes in dust, leather, olives.

People pass her, nodding.

"*Signora*", a sweep of the cloak.

Lily smiles.

"*Buona sera.*"

She can almost dance. Her feet are so light.

"*Signora Dalriada.*"

She moves, practically swaying, around the rim of the cathedral.

It is somewhere along the via del Proconsolo that her stomach knots. The Bargello prison is again before her. She remembers the boy hanging from the window, the cold winter air as they stood below.

Signora Dalriada.

She shivers.

The man in the brown cloak. They are here. In here.

They know.

Lily remembers all the times she ever hid. Tricking an imaginary sister into counting to a hundred as Lily ran all the way to the park swings, then imagining that sister — who was always a little smaller, a little friendlier — imagining her searching the streets in vain, missing Lily, and finding her at last. The ride on the see-saw in the cool August evening.

Lily hiding in her grandparents' field, the uncut hay high around her, wild strawberries deep at the tickly roots. She hears her name being called for lunch, hears them and sees them through the dusty hay. She cannot believe it. She is invisible. Delicious, delicious, to see and not be seen, to walk lightly upon pavement with no footsteps following after. Her grandmother's sun hat as it turns back to the house.

To disappear into the nothingness of another body, sinking down into the moss of a consciousness not your own, trying out the sofas and pressing at the boundaries, peering out through the luminous jelly of the eyes.

Yes. And to feel your body flow from your body, your little breathing boat of dreams heading out into the world, and you are looking up religiously and charting by the stars.

And the broom closets and the back rooms, the extra zero in the computer program, and your imaginary sister still counting: seventy-five, seventy-six. And the Angel's wings like a cloak of blessed numbness, ruffle, disappear my child, come inside, rest your bones. The air spangled and forgotten.

They have come.

How will she know when or whom?

Lily realizes she has never really peered into someone's eyes for the purpose of determining whether these eyes or that smile belongs to someone who might harm her. Suddenly everyone looks suspicious, the woman scolding her children by the road, the goldsmith in the window wrapping his bracelets. Is it this man approaching, his hat slightly askew, a slight limp in his step? He looks at her strangely enough but is soon on his awkward way.

Where do you run to run away? Lily careens down the via Proconsolo and nearly throws herself into the doors of the Badia Church. Tiny. Safe. Quiet. A crypt of someone in the corner.

It didn't matter.

This stunned her.

It didn't matter that two days ago this world didn't exist to her. It didn't matter that it was a trick of light or an atom count by Galileo.

This is it.

She paces the small church, a shaft of light trained on her back. She thought she had run away, coming here. Lily sits at the foot of the altar.

Turns out it was just another world.

Reality on your retina, Bernie's credo.

She hears the church bell. It is time.

> *Dies irae, dies illa,*
> *Solvet saeclum in favilla*

She has banded with a group of women, holy women. They will go to the church of Santissima Annunziata to venerate the image of the "Madonna Annunziata."

The panel was painted by an angel, an angel guiding the hand of the sleeping Bartolomeo. The Virgin is surrounded by silver: candlesticks, lamps, reliquaries. She is not particularly beautiful, this Madonna. She is plain beside the scrolled adornments.

This is the church of the wax people. Votive figures of the worthy dead of Florence, they live on inside these walls, their eerie stares and struck poses queerly flickering in the candlelight. They are the work of the *Fallimmagini*, the Imagemakers, who work in a shop in the city. They make the dead real again.

Lily nods. They are just like Bernie.

Lily crosses herself and moves in procession with the women. There is such a chill here, it is no wonder the faithful stand in religious clumps in all of the paintings. One young girl who can't be more than fifteen walks as Lily's companion as they proceed along the Stations of the Cross. Her eyes are downcast; she wears a plain scarf on her head. She is lovely in a pale way, like Beatrice is, young in the world.

They are about to enter a cloister.

"Chiostro dei Morti", someone intones.

Cloister of the Dead.

Lily breathes in the cold walls, incense wafted on stone. Andrea del Sarto is buried here. So is the murderous Cellini. The women mutter prayers to themselves. Lily falls back and pauses as they enter the chapel. The vision of them disappearing into the womb of the church, into the Cloister of the Dead, is too much.

No.

She backs away and turns, only to see the young girl with her. The girl's face betrays nothing. Lily begins walking toward the door of the church; the girl walks beside her.

They are in the Piazza, Lily fascinated by the little babies on the building to the left of Santissima Annunziata. Lily points up at them. The young woman nods.

"Spedale degli Innocenti," the girl says, making a rocking motion with her arms.

Yes, the foundling hospital. Bernie had mentioned it, said he thought he had come from one, said he thought we had all come from the Hospital of Unwanted Children. Little terracotta babies enamelled white, on the bluest of backgrounds, like little mummies, swaddled to death before they ever had a chance.

"Andrea della Robbia," the girl volunteers, pointing at the babes.

It is an exquisite Renaissance building, and the babies, too, are beautiful. And it is all for the unwanted offspring of the careless Florentines. Lily thinks of the Neonatural Institutes, the chrome and the rubbing alcohol. Her eyes blur. The tiny white babies look like filaments inside blue Christmas lights.

The women have returned and Lily and the girl join them. They are on their way to minister to the sick. Three of the women — Lily, the young girl, and an old woman called Maria — have entered the home of Giovanna Benetti. Her name is passed back and forth as the women cross themselves. They are not alone in their ministrations. The barber-surgeon is already there and with his assistant is about to bloodlet the woman.

Lily stands to the side, as does Maria and the girl. They cannot interfere with this official procedure. Already the man has applied *rottori*, evil-smelling unguents, to the *bubo* beneath the woman's arm.

THE PLAGUE SAINT   83

He has furthered the purification process by scratching glass along the *bubo* and pouring something that smells like onion juice onto the grated wounds. But for the *bubo* between her thighs, he will bloodlet at the ankle.

It is the *Fontana*. He will perform the Fountain. The assistant opens a pouch and removes the cutting glass, the razor blade. The glass is placed at the ankle and the razor slices. Blood flows, a red fountain. The woman swoons. Lily is about to leap forward but Maria's arm holds her back.

Giovanna's face is visionary. What is she seeing?

When the flow lessens, the barber-surgeon takes three leeches from a small sack. He applies the leeches to the wound. The assistant, who has disappeared into the back of the house, returns with a pigeon. The barber-surgeon slits it crosswise and cups it over the leeches.

The men speak to Maria and approach the stove with her. The barber-surgeon shows Maria something from his bag. Lily can't get a good look at it, but it is gold-coloured and looks vaguely like a railway spike. Then the man lifts an iron pole leaning up beside the stove, examines it, and nods. The men pack up their belongings and, without another glance at the woman, leave the house. Lily looks at the young girl by her side. The girl's face is ashen; yet she blinks through clear eyes and does not cry.

Now that the officials have gone, Maria comes alive, spitting orders to the girl and to Lily. Lily can understand the simple commands accompanied as they are by huge descriptive movements. She is to boil water. Lily looks around for a source and spots a large urn in the corner of the kitchen. She ladles some water into a pot and sets it on the fire. The young girl, whom Maria has addressed as Caterina, is scrubbing down the sides of the bed and laying out clean clothing. A lace-trimmed shirt, ragged, a slip with stains. A linen towel.

Horrible, when the woman opens her eyes. They are blank, just like the eyes of the woman in that old movie Lily saw when she was a kid. She never forgot the eyes of the young woman they were burning as a witch. And the man in the movie noticing them, too, and Lily feeling that she and that man had something in common. *The Seventh Seal*. She remembers. Remembers waiting for the seals to arrive.

Lily looks into her young companion's eyes. "Caterina?"

"*Si?*"

But she has no words.

Lily cannot believe it. Hasn't this woman, this Giovanna, been through enough? Lily doesn't know why but she thought that Maria had been sympathetic to the woman's suffering. She certainly didn't seem pleased with the barber-surgeon. And yet, here she is approaching the bed. Caterina is to hold the arm above the woman's head. Lily is to drape herself across the woman's body to keep her from kicking. Maria works swiftly, bringing the hot iron close to the *bubo*.

"*Grazie a Dio*", she inhales and presses the end of the pole into the *bubo*. The woman seizes and passes out.

"Thank God," Lily mutters and catches Caterina's quick glance.

The woman is washed, and Maria prepares a salve at the table. It is repulsive, like filthy wool. She pours fatty oil over it and kneads it. When it has become soft, like the guts of an old mattress, Maria places it over the various wounds on the woman's body. Lily smells the mixture. Familiar. She remembers. Sheep's wool. Fat, oil. Lily smiles. Lanolin. Maria has made lanolin.

The woman is dressed in clean garments and Caterina sits beside her, patting her forehead with a cloth. Maria tidies up the table and returns with a rosary.

Giovanna Benetti will not have to drink the cedar syrup. She will not have to swallow vinegar. The little tub of unguents the barber-surgeon has left has been put aside. Instead, Maria will administer the oil of white lilies. She will apply pork fat after a while, and they will pray.

Later, much later it seems, there is a sound at the door. Maria tries to rise from her knees but struggles until Lily assists her. Caterina goes to the door. Two of the other women have joined them, one carrying a large bowl covered by a dark blue cloth. The other women immediately make the sign of the cross, Caterina included. After a pause, Lily does the same. What new element is this, Lily wonders. Another unguent made of excrement, crushed glass and turpentine?

It is mushy, pale and almost colourless, like dishwater or thin thin oatmeal. Oatmeal soup?

Almost. Lily smells. Bread?

Bread soup.

Maria pulls her away. Apparently Lily is not to touch; this soup is blessed somehow. Have they had the priest bless it? Maria spoons it into a small bowl. Giovanna is roused and the women sit around her. One holds her head up slightly while another holds a clean napkin beneath her chin. Maria then allows the soup to dribble from the spoon into Giovanna's mouth. The other women begin telling the beads.

What is so important about the soup? Could this be one of the saint's cures?

Caterina is watching Lily this time.

This has taken hours, yet the women do not seem tired, although Maria's hip is getting worse. They are finally ready to leave. It has been the strangest time. Lily feels something important has happened here, but she is at a loss to explain what. Belief? Lily did not believe in the treatment by the barber-surgeon, but then neither did she believe in Maria's hot iron and salve cure. Prayers? The holy soup?

Caterina waits for her in the street.

"Mangia?" she asks.

Lily must look confused because the girl makes eating motions with her hand.

"Si...si!" Lily responds.

They are breaking Tuscan bread and spooning beans into deep bowls. Caterina says nothing. Lily watches her move around this kitchen she seems to know so well. The rooms are small but not that small. And she is still a child. Surely she must live with her family. Lily's eye travels the length of the room. No clothes drying by the stove. No shoes on the ledge.

But there, inside the entrance to the other room Lily has not explored, there is a hanging — toy? A mobile? Lily gets up and goes over to the doorway. Thin threads holding small wooden chips. They are shaped like fish. They don't look like real fish. Poorly etched; eyes that fish wouldn't have. An amateur job, to be sure. But their shadows! The wood chips have caught the candlelight from the kitchen and above these stiff effigies the shadows of real fish move. It is as if Lily is underwater, looking up at fish that are closer to the surface. They move with such grace, these celestial fish.

How lovely. Planned, executed for a little child's whimsy or wonder? She wishes she could ask Caterina. Lily turns back to the kitchen and sees Caterina point and then the world disappears.

*

Bernie was there like a long-lost relative huddled in the corner of a train station. He approached her as if, perhaps, he could barely recognize her, as if he were trying to remember what coat she was wearing when she left town so many years before. All those old movies beginning, ending, with a train. All those hopefuls waiting at stations for people who did not come home.

His eyes were bloodshot. He was in his underwear. How long had she been gone? It was like that old favourite of her father's, *The Time Machine*. Rod Taylor nudging forward in time, looking in wonder at the changes to his house and to his street before pitching headlong into the future. Lily, on the other hand, had leaned backward on the crystal handle, and look where she had been.

Except it didn't feel like that. Except she didn't feel as if she was home. She had just been sitting in Caterina's kitchen, she was still hungry for the beans. Where was Caterina? Where were the women and Giovanna Benetti? Was Giovanna well; does she get well?

"So, you've sampled the waters," Bernie said, a small grin that looked almost sad.

"What?" Lily had to focus.

"Uhm...excuse me, but I couldn't help but notice a certain enjoyment factor in your latest adventure."

Oh, God. Taddeo. There was nothing she could say. She stared at him.

"Am I right or am I right? It *is* better in there, eh? *Hungry Night!*"

The room was airless and cool. She could not feel the sun. She was home, all right.

"I heard from Roland. He thinks you'll have to move. He thinks they know where you are."

Lily stood at the cloudy window.

"I'm not going," she said, as something that might be a falling leaf or a bird passed by her view.

"Lily, c'mon, it's hard enough keeping one step — "

"Bernie, they know. Okay? They're in there," she pointed to the operations room. "They can take me anytime. I'm not running anymore."

"I don't want them to take you, Saint Lily."

Bloodshot eyes that were welling. "Look, shit, a *lot* of work, I mean, a lot of people have laid their asses on the line for you — "

"Exactly. And I don't want any more to have to. Look, I'm beginning to think that you get what you get, you know? For some reason, I get to do this. And you — " she tapped a finger on his chest, " — you get to make the tea and help me plan my next entry."

"You're going back in? Use your head! Which one is it in there? What do they look like? There's no way I can let you go back!"

"So what am I going to do? Sit here and wait for them? Or hide in a sewage pipe? Face it, they know how to find me. I can't let them get to me up here," she raised a finger to her forehead. "So I'll meet them, out here or in there. I'll dance as long as there's music, okay, Bernie?"

A look passed between them, one Lily had not seen in a long time. Lily thought, in fact, that it no longer existed. It was trust. She trusted Bernie. He trusted her.

Caterina would wonder where she disappeared to, wouldn't she? Lily didn't know how that worked. Wouldn't they wonder? Would it be viewed as miraculous, Lily's sudden vanishing? She wanted to ask Bernie but she was too tired. So, after tea and a grilled cheese sandwich Lily stretched out on her cot and closed her eyes on the grey room.

When she awoke Bernie was gone. Lily searched the operations room and glanced in his bedroom. Of course, he did have to go out sometime if only to meet a customer since he could no longer meet them here. And he had to get food.

It was funny. Lily had started forgetting those essential chores — groceries, dusting — the very stuff she did for a living not so long ago. Food just appeared, as did places to lay her head. Which scared her. From what she'd read about ascetics and holy people they had a seeming disregard for the essentials of life. The Franciscans waited for food to arrive. They were not allowed to beg. They stood at bus stops until someone paid their fare. They simply trusted that the Lord would provide. And if the Lord came in the guise of a hotel clerk or — God forbid — a purveyor of virtual porn, well, there were a lot of wonders under the sun, that was all.

Bernie had left some printouts on the kitchen table. They would have to be more interesting than the three movie books, which she'd been through a couple of times by now.

Lily's heart jumped.

The papers concerned the saint.

So, Bernie had managed to tap into the Church's confidential files! Lily's hand shook as she picked up the papers.

Domenica da Paradiso. Domenica...of Paradise?

She came from a town called Paradiso, on the Ripoli plain.

Unfortunately, most of the text was in Italian and Latin. She would have to ask for Bernie's help. Lily had only the most basic Latin, and this only because of the Alchemy Club. Bernie spoke contemporary Italian and had a smattering of Latin from school. "Latin!" Another thorn in his trucker dad's side.

It was maddening to have the papers so close and to be forced to wait for Bernie. The top page held a few facts

The woman was a Dominican nun. She founded a convent. She had been dead almost eighty years when the canonization hearings began.

But wasn't that the way it usually worked? Lily was no expert on sainthood, but didn't it have to happen later on, like a certain number of years *after* death? There was a lot of paperwork; there were witnesses and testimonies. There had to be documented miracles.

Lily knew that the Church of the Survivors was arranging for her miracles. She also knew that they wanted a live saint. But for how long? It was the old Frank Buck theme: *Bring 'Em Back Alive!*, which Lily's father had appended to his "Stayin' Alive" credo. Bring 'Em Back Alive. Right. But for how long?

Bernie, where the hell was Bernie? She could do without the shepherd's pie. C'mon. Lily paused. *C'mon.* That was Bernie! He moved around in this world as if he almost belonged here. It stunk, he would probably tell you it stunk, but he could live with the odour and, besides, he'd figured out a way to make a living.

It was strange how quiet the rooms were. She could plug into any place, any fantasy. She could be anywhere she wanted. Except with Beatrice. Except fingering her daughter's hair, her real daughter's real hair.

Lily sat at the counter with a piece of paper and a pen. She remembered doing this as a child, sitting in the empty kitchen waiting for her parents to get home from work. She had a little desk with a matching chair, and her tape recorder was set up beside it, but she preferred listening to the hum of the refrigerator as she drew pictures or wrote letters to her aunts and uncles and grandparents. Who sometimes wrote back. There was a distinct thrill to seeing the letters fly through the slot, mail from nowhere, it seemed, letters magically produced from the air. And then, occasionally, something addressed to her.

Miss Lily Dalriada

Her grandparents, or her Auntie Bet or, especially strange, her Uncle Philly.

Hey, Chodio Babe: (from her childhood pronunciation of *Cheerios*. Would he never forget?)

Hey, Chodio Babe:

> *How's it going? Got your letter and you sound just*
> *fine. Life up here in the mountains is really really good.*
> *Thinking of buying some land near Field and —*

And. And. Other lives going on out there, whispered through the mail slot's thin metal lips.

Before she could begin to compose anything, Bernie returned with a bag of groceries.

"I was in touch with some people. I had to go there. Too risky to call or anything. They said they'd take you if we left tonight."

"Bernie."

"No, listen. Listen. I've been thinking. You can't stay here. It's just suicide to sit here and wait. I can take you to them tonight and, who knows, we might come up with something."

"Bernie." Lily took the bag from his arms and sat him down. "I trust you, Bernie. I know you won't make me do this. I think we both realize — "

She started pulling groceries from the bag.

"I think that's why there's all this great food. *Look at this!* I haven't seen sour-cream, paprika, in ages!"

Bernie smiled in spite of himself. "You don't know what I had to promise the guy to get this stuff. Let's just say, he won't have to feel

Elvis's pulse to know he's alive."

Lily arranged the groceries on the table. "This is going to make a really fine dinner." She looked up. "Thank you, Bernie."   He smiled as he cleared the table. The papers had been moved. He picked them up without a word.

Even prisoners used to get a last meal, choosing what to put into their systems one last time. Tomato sauce gives me the cramps. O, God. An insane little giggle. Cantaloupe makes me burp. The etiquette of the condemned.

Would it end tonight? Bernie's urgent actions, the formality of the supper preparation. Lily would know, wouldn't she? She had always believed that she would have a sense, an advance warning, of her demise. It was why she could never quite buy these stories about people who suddenly keeled over dead, or who were swept away in their cars in a sudden Texas flash flood. A typhoon in Bangladesh taking out a thousand people in a moment. A whole village. That never made any sense to Lily. Surely all one thousand would pause, look up or out or just intently at their hands, stunned, as the revelation came upon them. And if there were a thousand of them, wouldn't they try to act? Build a shelter, something?

"Bernie, could you help me go back in?"

I want to come in. Please, Mama. Banging on the screen door. The Gates of Paradise.

"Maybe. Maybe later. We'll deal with it all later. I think you should rest first."

And out of his pocket he pulled a small pouch of bubble bath.

"Where did you get this?"

Truly impressed with Bernie's abilities. Such luxuries were only available to the rich. When Lily had cleaned houses, she would sometimes take a whiff of one of the oils or sachets. The smell was always exotic, the flowers from another part of the world, from another world altogether, one Lily wouldn't travel to.

Bernie found a knife and Lily slit the end of the pouch. An aroma explosion.

"Oh!"

"I even cleaned the bathtub before I left. It's waiting."

A sweep of his arm. His hands on her shoulders. "Go."

She lay back in the tub. She had been extravagant, squeezing the entire contents into the water. And she filled the tub far higher than she would have done normally. There was a sense of abandon in the exercise and Lily found herself revelling in the warm sudsy water that smelled of a tropical island. At least, she thought it did. She would read the papers with him that evening. And then she would go back inside.

She thought again about the meal he was preparing. Yes, she could understand now, ordering peas instead of corn. Sending the steak back to be turned one more time. Because you might be dead in an hour or two but you were alive right now and you liked it medium rare.

Candlelight.
"Oh, Bernie...."
Linen. Linen!
"It was my mother's."
Everything was lovely. Lily remembered when such things were possible. They still were possible for the very rich. Lily counted tablecloths when she cleaned their homes. She polished silver. Babies had silver dishes.
"Well, why don't you sit down?"
A little too nervous, too jerky, to have made an admirable head waiter, but the conscientious service was there.
"Bernie, is that a rose?"
Over on the counter in a vase.
"Oops, forgot. Well, almost. It's silk. I usually give one to the bride when I hand over her honeymoon program, sort of a nice touch, you know."
"Sorry I asked. Though, I guess, if the sex isn't real why should the flower be?"
He looked crestfallen.
"Sorry. It's nice. Really."

He poured some wine, apologizing for the quality. Lily knew it was next to impossible to get any decent wine anymore.
"Just plonk. But in my mother's *Cross and Olives*."
"What are we toasting?"
Bernie handed her a glass and held his by two fingertips, swirling the contents.
"Saints. Oh, and sinners."

RITA DONOVAN

Domenica and me, Lily thought.

They clicked glasses.

"This is where the bride and groom have to kiss."

"What?"

"You know, in weddings. They click glasses and — "

"I thought it was when they clink glasses. With a spoon." Lily demonstrated.

"Oh. Oh, yeah." He seemed almost agitated.

"Bernie, do you know something I don't? Is the pasta booby-trapped? Is the door going to burst open and the Council storm in?"

"No...no! Jesus, what do you think I am? I got a dinner going, here. I'm gonna put the salad out, okay? And the garlic bread."

She couldn't tell whether he was just annoyed or he had a serious nervous disorder. He jittered around the room organizing dishes, placing the salad bowl on the table and carefully — carefully — arranging the serving forks atop it.

"Eat. *Mangia, mangia.*"

Lily paused. Caterina had asked her to eat.

"I hope I get some food this time," she said.

"What?"

Lily lifted some salad into her bowl.

"This is great, Bernie. You really went all out."

"What 'til you taste my manicotti."

Bernie put on soft music in the background but abruptly rose in the middle of a quiet samba and switched it off. The next thing Lily was listening to was Gregorian chants.

"I like it. Relaxing," Bernie said. "Okay with you?"

It was so familiar. It could not have been more familiar to her if it had had a disco beat and falsetto voices. That music. The Church of Santa Croce. The Church of Santa Maria Novella. The little church Matteo's wife was buried from.

"You okay? What, too spicy?"

Matteo and Maria and Caterina. Taddeo with the stomach muscles of Michelangelo's slave. Salty. Bread and salt. Bread soup.

Lily ate Bernie's meal, glancing up to smile or gesture. Bernie complied with the tenor of the evening, bringing a tiramisu to the table without so much as a word.

Lily thanked him and offered to clean up but he refused.

"I got coffee brewing. Sit back and relax."

Then it was time to look at the documents.

Bernie checked the locks and leaned a chair up against the door. He glanced at Lily. Nervous laughter escaped them both.

Then he sat down to look at the printouts.

"The Latin I'm not good with. I told you I only took it as an option course. Spent all my time in the media lab. But, here goes. *Domenica da Paradiso*. Domenica of the town of Paradiso."

"I know that much."

"C'mon, I'm just getting warmed up, here."

Lily listened as Domenica's life unfolded. Born in 1473, she lived to be 80. She founded a convent, had predictions, and offered relief to the town during another, earlier plague. Not bad for 80 years.

Domenica, the beautiful young peasant girl who was always 'different'. The child who had caused her mother no discomfort during pregnancy and delivery. The child who, herself, never cried, who never played with other children but prayed constantly. The child who ate but once a day.

The young girl who was so lovely, who was being forced by her family to marry, whose two jealous sisters threatened to charge her with witchcraft. Two wicked sisters, just like in the fairy tales. The sister Angela who tried to poison her. The sister Filippa who accused her of adultery with a priest. And the two of them dying of appropriate diseases: Angela, the poisoner, of stomach trouble; Filippa, the liar, of cancer of the tongue.

The Domenica of the visions.
Flaming red willows in a dark winter world.
The seasons, the seasons.
Sticks of burning wood.

The Domenica of the cloister, the convent of Crocetta.
The Domenica who in 1499 moved to the city of *Firenze*.

Lily wondered whether Domenica had shaken, too, when she first stepped into Florence. She was 26 years old then; it was the year before the new century. She was about the same age Lily had been at the millennium, when the craziness was all around her, everybody childish and afraid, hushed whispers as the last few seconds ticked down.

And here was Domenica walking into a bustling Florentine street to become a servant in a great house. Did she wonder, then, did she suspect that her life would turn out the way it did? She had always been different, perhaps she did know she'd been chosen.

Was she a good servant?

How could you be a good servant if all you did was pray the whole day long?

"The testimony says here an angel, a guardian angel, did the housework while Domenica prayed."

Now that was the idea. A guardian angel who did windows! Lily stifled a chuckle.

Domenica would soon begin her small convent. It seemed to be a question of getting a house and taking in women.

"You said she was a servant? Where's she going to get a house?"

From the dreams.

So much done with dreams, so much store put in them. Changing your life because of a dream. Lily could not imagine —

Domenica had dreamed of Saint Catherine, her calm intensity, her presence. In the dream, Catherine handed Domenica the clothes of Saint Dominic. From this day forward, and initially without permission, Domenica would wear the robes of the Dominican order. When she did receive permission from the order it was with the provision that she wear a large red cross on the front of the robe. Scarlet letter. Red crucifix. It was a way of keeping things simple.

Lily tried to remember significant or, at least, vivid dreams that she'd had. There was the baseball dream when she was a kid. It had signified the end of her interest in the Blue Jays. There were the dreams about her mother in the hospital, her father in the home. There were the brilliant flash-card dreams she had while she was giving birth, Lily and Beatrice — or the child who was about to become Beatrice — sitting in a clearing on the side of a mountain, looking down into a valley of larch trees.

Had any of it meant anything? What was she supposed to do, become a hospital orderly? Grow trees in the deserted parks? And yet, here this woman woke up one morning and put on a nun's habit and changed her future.

The women came together and began doing handiwork: weaving,

sewing, embroidering. They started selling their fabrics and garments. Seven years later, Domenica had saved 100 *scudi.*

"What's a *scudi* get you?"

"Who knows?" Bernie shrugged. "But it says she bought land for the convent with 191 *scudi.*"

"Land grab. How did she do it?"

"Get this," Bernie pointed enthusiastically, "it says that an angel brought the extra cash. Did the nun have connections or what!"

Her angels were certainly proficient. They always knew what to bring. Not like the year's supply of paper products Lily's Uncle Philly had won, "and not a rolling paper in sight!" Not the angel who didn't show up when Lily's mother was taking that faulty transfusion.

"You gotta have the right angels," Bernie nodded.

Lily had the ice-cave Angel, the glacial angel with the thick frozen wings.

"It says here that 100 sequins turned into 50,000 *scudi.* That's how they got the convent."

"SEQUINS!"

Bernie smiled and shook his head. "Who'd have figured? Elvis was right. Actually," he added, "I hate to break the spell, but I think a sequin was some kind of coin back then." He paused again. "Elvis has left the building."

Bernie read for a while. Then Lily got up and paced. The chair was still crooked against the door. There was still the problem of waiting.

"Please, Bernie, I want to go in once more. Maybe I can find this Domenica."

"Not unless you enter earlier. Don't forget, she's been dead a lot of years by now. Then."

"I mean, to learn about her hearings. Maybe I can find out something. Anything. Bernie, this could be me any day now."

Bernie exhaled, defeated, and pointed down the hall.

"Just don't wear sequins, okay? Somebody would probably hold you for ransom."

Lily tried not to panic as she prepared herself. She wasn't looking, after all, for a way out, was she? There was no pressure on her to avoid anything. Was there?

Just go in. Just be there.

Lily took a deep breath, and exhaled it in Firenze.

*

Where is she? Lily feels a surge of adrenalin as she tries to orient herself, where is...there...the Duomo...the centre. Okay.

Via dei Servi. She is in front of the shop of the *Fallimmagini*. Wax faces stare out at her, eyeless...no, not eyeless. Visionless. Blank gazes looking through windows onto the street.

Lily pushes open the door. Darker inside than she expected. A workroom at the back. The place is crowded with pale people of different sizes, but these are not people, she reminds herself; these are not alive. Yet she can see one of them moving, she is sure of it. Another shot of adrenalin.

Lily stares into each pair of eyes in turn. One pair stares back.

"*Signore*," Lily sighs.

"*Si...si*," he moves out from behind a waxwork figure he has been touching up.

"*Signore*", Lily says again, relieved.

He guides her over to the corner of the shop. There is a row of gouty-looking men; public officials perhaps? There is a well-dressed young girl, obviously the daughter of some nobleman. There is a statue of a woman in a gown. He turns it in Lily's direction.

Lily gasps.

She is staring at herself. The man smiles, taking her shock as a compliment. It is almost life-size, three-quarters, maybe three-quarters. Weren't people shorter then? Aren't they?

Lily Dalriada is going to hang in the Church of Santissima Annunziata with the other wax humans, suspended in the incense in the flickering dark.

No.

"*No...signore!*"

"*Si, si!*" he cries, rather impatient now. The *Fallimmagini* proffers the staring image, "*Vaghezza, leggiadria.*"

Lily tears from the shop, races down the via dei Servi. Somewhere else, somewhere....

She is out of breath by the time she reaches the Piazza del Duomo. Panting. Two women give her sidelong glances as she tries to catch her breath. A boy with a horrible burn scar on his face comes by half-carrying, half-dragging a basket of chestnuts. He sees Lily slumped against the cathedral wall, reaches into the basket and scoops up a grubby handful of chestnuts. As he approaches Lily, a smile appears across his scarred features.

"Prego."

Lily's hand and the boy's hand touch gently.

The city passes by. Men, members of the nobility, barber-surgeons, public health officials. One person Lily is sure must be a grave-digger, because the entire crowd freezes as one person as he moves among them.

Yes. The sound of his ankle bell.

Lily watches a while longer, rolling a chestnut in her palm.

She begins walking in the direction the grave-digger has taken. It is easy to keep him in sight because people mark a wide berth around him. Lily, too, remains a good distance back. Where is he going? A plague hospital? A cemetery? How is she going to find the saint like this?

The women had known about the saint, Lily was sure of that. Something muttered as they administered the bread soup, something about the bread soup. She should go back to Giovanna.

She could go back to that house. But, and this strikes Lily as a desperate thought, somehow she is afraid that if she returns to the house, Giovanna will not be there. Not that she will have been moved. Not that she will have died, although Lily knows that this is how entire families disappeared during the plague, one moment bustling through a house and the next — empty space in a deserted set of rooms, a white cross painted on the door. But not that she will have died. Simply, that she will not ever have existed at all.

Oh, the future has its own little twists, she wishes to warn these people. Here, you might die in one another's arms, but at least you remember one another's arms. In the future, Lily shivers, in her own time, a person can cease to exist without more effort than the click of a computer key.

It is how Lily will not exist, except as written up by the Church of the Survivors.

How Beatrice will be forced to read the testimony of the life of a saint named Lily Dalriada.

How Beatrice's Mama will have disappeared.

Lily follows the grave-digger. A man beside her has crossed himself and uttered the word, "*monatto.*"

What an image this is. In neither time would its significance be missed. A condemned woman pursuing the dragger of infected corpses. The grave-diggers were thought to spread the plague. Of course they were feared; revered? Held in awe. They were condemned, too; condemned prisoners, most of them, given the choice of the job and possible death, or the sentence of certain death. A grim laugh escaped one of them as he was propositioned.

So they moved corpses. And were good at their jobs, the ones who survived for any length of time, that is. Turnover was high. Another guttural laugh. But those who didn't perish immediately became...immortal? Immune?

For some reason, did not perish.

And they wielded great power, these men. They could throw your beloved wife or husband to the dogs. They could collect the liquid poisons expelled from your dead brother's body and sell it as a cure, or as a poison, depending on the market. They could defile the still-living creatures they were carting to the open unconsecrated fields outside the city.

"*Dio, Dio,*" the faint voice of a man even more damned than the *monatto.*

God have mercy.

The grave-digger and his accomplice stripping the man before tossing him, still breathing, into the shallow grave. Lime clumping over the man's startled eyes. The clothes appearing later at the stall of the rag merchant, the *rigattieri* proffering clothing at one time so cherished, handed down in wills:

> 2 linen shirts, one with lace
> 2 lace collars
> 1 damask tablecloth, red
> 1 veil
> 1 cloak with enamel clasp

In the humid air, the clothes of the dead sit in heaps, the air heavy around them. A dog runs through the street with the arm of a man. The ragged fingers brush the edge of the shirt the arm once wore.

The grave-diggers believed that if you were afraid, the Bad Disease would enter you and kill you. They moved among the retching, decaying citizens of Firenze, touching them, carting them, without taking any precautions. Some of them died. These were the afraid.

Live in fear and you die, they grin, donning the pants of the deceased victim, pulling on the cloak that hid the festering *bubo*.

She has lost sight of the *monatto*. Has he entered one of the houses? Lily slows her steps and is about to move out into the street when, as if it has been rehearsed, a door opens. Lily blinks. It is not the grave-digger who emerges but a member of the *Miseracordia*, the robe and hood concealing the identity, as always. Does the man live here in this not rich, not poor, area of town? Does he have a wife, and children who also hear the church bell and then watch their father rise from the table and don the robes so he can enter the street in search of the sick or dying?

In Lily's time he would be a superhero, a Spiderman or a Batman, a member of the latest galaxy protectorate. Because certainly he faced the same dangers as the *monatto*, squatting beside a body that had been thrown out into the road, lifting it onto the litter and carrying it away. The foam from the mouth could adhere to his robe, to his leg.

Who is this man who volunteers to stand, unnamed, before Death, before the Plague Virgin? Why does he do it? For the selfishness of his immortal soul? Was the rotting cadaver beside him merely a conduit to the man's everlasting peace?

Still. And even if. The *monatto* had avoided certain death to play this game of roulette. The member of the *Miseracordia* had not. The hood, the red robe, the white crucifix on the front. The figure pauses, or seems to pause for he moves so fluidly. The robe flaps behind him as he hurries down the street.

Something is happening in this street. First the *monatto*, then the *Miseracordia*, and now this horse and wagon rounding the corner. When it stops, two men climb off. They are wearing white cloaks with red crosses on them. They have chosen a specific door further up the street and they enter it with buckets, tubes, and other paraphernalia. A woman pokes her head out a window to the right of Lily's head, utters a curse, and slams the window shut.

Lily tries to get closer to the house. People are creeping by in an arc around it, making the sign of the cross. Then she smells it. Sulphur. Fumigators. Lily coughs and backs away. This is an infected house. She had not until now seen the white cross marking the door.

Furniture is being kicked and dragged into a pile in front of the house. Curtains, a small cabinet, a few chairs. A table now, a child's doll caught in the warp and weft of a loom. If only there had been books, and mirrors. And silk to add to the pile. Savonarola would have been proud.

Where is the child who talked to this doll? The woman who worked the loom? The sound of crockery hitting the cobblestones. The crunch as someone steps on yellow glass that had just been a pitcher with flowers.

These men are surely going to die of the fumes. Lily watches as they hoist an upholstered chair atop the heap. Something clinks to the ground. Lily sees one of the men pick up a chain. A silver cross sways from it. The man flips the crucifix up, paws it, and slips it into his pocket.

She has lost both the *monatto* and the *Miseracordia*. She is unfamiliar with these streets. Are they heading toward the convent of Santa Maria Novella? Lily wishes she knew where the canonization hearings were taking place. Perhaps one of the sisters at the Dominican order might know. Where is the Convent of Crocetta anyway? Bernie had said it out of town.

Lily rounds the corner at the via Della Bella Donne. She cannot shake the feeling that she is being followed. One moment she is the pursuer, the next she is the one being followed. Well, okay. Lily slows to a stop and backs against the wall.

Watch yer back.

Sheriff Galileo opening the saloon door with the tip of his *Winchester*. The barrel of his *Colt*. With the tip of his snub-nosed revolver.

Oh, Sheriff, thank the Lord you came back.

Just doin' my job, Ma'am.

Lily almost cries when she sees it is Caterina. She wants to run up and hug her. This is the first time any of Lily's visitations have overlapped.

"Caterina," she beams, holding out her hand.

"Si...Si. Buon giorno."

The girl seems even paler than before. Lily is struck by the thought that Caterina may be sick, that she may also have to suffer like Giovanna Benetti. She is struck by how much the thought bothers her. She takes a chance. "Domenica...*Domenica da Paradiso?*" she whispers. "*Dove?*"

Yes. Where is it that you keep your long-dead bodies that even now perform miracles?

But Caterina does not look puzzled. Her clear eyes seem to read exactly what Lily is saying, for she is taking her by the arm and leading her through the street.

Lily obliges and the women look, possibly, like any number of other women strolling arm in arm through the alleyways of Firenze, the sound of light steps barely registering on the cobbles and the large flat stones.

Lily has been avoiding one thought. She first had it when she emerged from the last adventure. She realized how she had come to count on Bernie. She knew that this was the DNA of friendship. Without any absolute proof, she had decided to trust Bernie. Had she similarly come to trust this Caterina who it was not even possible to know?

Caterina pauses at the corner of a street. A tiny piazza directly ahead. A terracotta shop in the alley. Is Caterina lost? *There ought to be little signs.* Uncle Philly nodding in the ozone.

Lily sits along the edge of a fountain and pushes her back up against the side.

The world goes blank.

GRID.

Oh, Jesus, what have I —

Dark. Evening. Where? When? Horrible, these torches, the light slick alongside all the faces. A parade through the street...this is...long ago. The smell!

It is a *Triumph.*

Lily blinks. She has heard of these.

Triumphs. Street theatre. Representations of the large truths. Firenze as Victor. The Lord as Victor.

But this.

This is the *Triumph of Death.*

Stick figures lead the way, riding decrepit horses. Following them, the huge buffalos snort and pull the black wagon adorned with bones. Lily does not want to guess to whom or what they belong.

And astride the wagon, Death. His scythe flashes in the torchlight. He has dominion over the coffins angled all around him on the cart.

The buffalos are fearsome in their plodding, their eyes flicker dumbly as the light falls across their faces.

The wagon stops.

The trumpets, the muffled drums, a drone as the coffins open. Lily wants to cover her ears and her eyes.

Black figures, white skeletons painted on them. Some sway, some dance. They chant something now that Lily does not understand. She makes out the word Death. And we. And you.

The parade starts moving. The black standards emblazoned with skulls, the flutter of the skulls.

> *Dies irae, dies illa*
> *Solvet saeclum in favilla*

Lily sees Caterina's face in the crowd just before the torch chokes and the smoke obscures her vision. She moves off the fountain. The image of the procession is burned onto her eyes as it flashes and disappears.

GRID.

Lily can still smell the smoke.

Caterina is asking a gentleman for directions. Or something.

Calm down, Lily.

See how calm Caterina is? She doesn't look upset at the strange sight they have just witnessed

It is only after Lily is quite long into the journey to the Convent of Crocetta that it occurs to her that Caterina should not have been present at the *Triumph of Death*.

Lily holds Caterina's arm and walks with her eyes closed, tripping over uneven intersections. She remembers the stories Bernie had read, stories about how Domenica had helped her city, at the time suffering from another plague, to unite and defend themselves against the Imperial Troops. How she had prayed for the body of the city to be spared in exchange for her own body. How she had offered her own blood in its place.

How Domenica's body was weakened by haemorrhages and fatigue. How doctors bloodlet her despite her anaemia. How her health was permanently altered by this bargain she had made with God.

How her city was spared.

Domenica da Paradiso, who would become a Medicean saint, who would be exhumed and studied and proclaimed.

Saint.

In Lily's time she would not have gotten past the visions. Her desires for pain and blood would have triggered a *Thorazine* or *Prozac* response. In Lily's time she would not have been holy.

Lily walks along the pathway to the convent. Caterina has stopped twice now, the second time to speak to an old woman by the roadside. A deal is being struck here, Lily thinks, and once again she watches Caterina closely.

Caterina speaks in whispers to the sister at the gate.

Lily enters the convent of Santa Croce. The *Crocetta.*

She covers her head. She should not be here. Lily doesn't know what Caterina has had to say to arrange this but, wordlessly, the two are led into the chapel. Strange, the feeling that she has done this before. She has listened to Bernie's translation of the canonization proceedings, but nothing has prepared her for this.

Doctors, cardinals, inquisitors, notaries, judges, the elder nuns. Lily and Caterina are huddled over to the side in the back. Lily is struck by the idea that if an artist were to paint this scene right now, there they would be, nameless and forever in the background of the great event taking place in the centre. The background boy in the children's book.

There are two tombs.

This proves the documents. The body was moved years after Domenica's death and placed in the second sepulchre. The first tomb has remained, adorned with a shield that portrays a skull and bones. Lily studies the painting hanging beside the sarcophagus. She cannot see it too clearly from where she is standing but it is too striking to turn away from.

A building in flames, billowing black smoke, the building surrounded by nuns, while the Virgin looks down on the scene from above. She is bathed in light, this Madonna.

Lily and Caterina follow behind the dignitaries as the life of Domenica is recorded.

Here are the cells she lived in, paintings depicting her life over the doorway. They are so simple:

— Domenica as a child talking to the Virgin Mary in a vineyard. She stands there, trowel in hand. She could be in Lily's grandparents' backyard. She could be in a park. Little red crucifixes hang from the vines.

— Domenica, older, being threatened by a serpent.

— Domenica, ill on her cot, with two saints by her side. Saint Magdalene. Saint Catherine. *Magdalena, Caterina*.

— The last painting depicts the Medici popes.

Simple.

— Lily in her grandparents' field hiding in the tall grass, among the wild strawberries. She is talking to the crickets.

— Lily watching her mother's body behind the glass. Her father is pressing his hand up to the pane.

— Lily holding a newborn Beatrice. Her face is bathed in light. Behind them both, a woman holds a paper that allows this child to be.

— Lily in the background now, the council of the Church of the Survivors in the centre looking out. Their eyes are the eyes of the wax statues hanging in the church of Santissima Annunziata.

This is the votive chapel.

This is it.

The gold silk blanket.

The blanket must be removed. Lily lets out a slight gasp at the sudden beauty. Beneath it is a painted image of the saint. She is in brilliant light; she is surrounded by angels and golden stars. An angel is handing Domenica a red cross.

"Nec non pluribus Angelis...circumdatam," the notary speaks and records this in his book.

The key to the sepulchre. It hangs from a red silk cord with a red stone attached. Lily watches the stone sway like a little metronome ticking away the metre of the centuries.

The body.

Lily is not sure she is ready for this. She looks over at Caterina.

Caterina?

Caterina is gone.

Okay, what now? How do you tactfully slip away from a canonization hearing? Lily presses herself further into the background.

A hothouse. A miniature hothouse, Lily thinks, as she looks through the crystal lid. Beneath it, amid flowers – roses, lilies – lies the saint. In a fleeting thought Lily wishes there had been flowers around her mother, instead of the bare rigid sheets.

White cloth. Black mantle. Red cross. Always the red cross. White veil, and over it a crown of silver and gold. Her arms are folded across her chest, a rosary in her hands. She rests under the crystal cover like Snow White waiting for her prince to ride by. Like Lily's mother had, while on the other side of the glass Lily's father shuffled the soft-shoe of the bereft.

There is a quiet taking of oaths. The physicians and the dignitaries are swearing to report truthfully everything they find.

Truthfully, My Lords, when the poison apple fell from her mouth she awakened and married the prince. Truthfully, the woman threw off her hospital gown, donned a sparkly dress and the couple danced away to the sound of "Stayin' Alive".

They will now investigate the body.

"Omnibus patentis."

And now the body of Domenica is being undressed. Off comes the veil, the mantle, the wimple, off comes the scapular, the habit. Off come the woollen slippers. Now there is merely a small piece of cloth covering the pubic region.

This body has not decayed. Lily is fascinated. It is long-dead, leathery. But it is entire. The face retains an expression Lily can only assume the nun once possessed. Lily pushes forward a little, moves to the right side. Yes, she is all here. Except for...her ears...and her finger is hanging off.

Relics?

August 14, 1533.

The sad frenzy when she died, the desire to retain a relic of this saintly woman, the ear of Domenica da Paradiso. The frenzy, Bernie had said, was a prerequisite to possible canonization.

The doctors lift and ease the body over, tapping the dry skin, weighing parts of the remains.

"Optime conservatum", the notary nods.

She looks like one of the wax people. For a moment Lily wonders whether that is all she is. But this would not explain the pinkish colour of the breasts. Almost alive, they are markedly different in colour from the rest of the body. And the heart. The heart seems swollen.

"*Aliquis tumor*", the notary pauses, writes, and pauses and writes again. Something that looks like blood is on the cloth that had covered the chest.

There are the scars of self-mutilation. Whip scars. Calluses. Years of the hair-shirt, the mattress filled with shells, the bleeding. The bloodletting. Bernie had said that she had been a beautiful young woman. She had had suitors but refused them.

"She tried to make herself ugly," he read. As a young girl, she whipped herself with leather and chains. Fasting. Choosing not to sleep. And yet she remained beautiful.

"When she was twenty-three, she asked God to turn her into something ugly," Bernie said.

God complied. She lost her colour, her weight, her ener-gy. "Like she was made of air," Bernie pointed to the text.

Lily looks down at the scarred wax woman. The nuns said that, after a time, the only food she took was the Holy Eucharist. The notary is in conference with the physicians. It is something about the heart. Domenica's heart.

This is the Swollen Heart.

This is the Sacred Heart visited upon the saintly body of Domenica da Paradiso.

This will be the Cult of the Swollen Heart.

It is the proof they have needed to proceed.

Signs of the cross, whisperings. A bell tolling somewhere.

The Cult of the Swollen Heart.

Domenica da Paradiso. The nuns are beside themselves with joy. Lily backs out of the chapel.

As she treads the road back to the city, she notices how overcast the sky has become. Oppressive grey, the air unmoving.

She does not want to be lying on a slab like Domenica, people poking her, prodding the skin on her arm for 'give', someone noting her stages of decay. The absolute truth — she pauses to examine a wildflower she has never seen before, pale orange with a yellow ring around it. The absolute truth is that she never wants to die. And even here, even on this dirt path by the road, she realizes how useless a thing this is to know. Any child who has ever sat at the top end of a see-saw knows this. And probably also knows that it is hopeless, feeling the air rush past the ears as the see-saw descends.

The old ones in the ManorHomes lining up to get at their mailboxes. Any message, anything on the terminal, any hand-scrawled note from the olden times? Fingers pawing gently inside the shiny metal box.

And one day, *The Triumph of Death*. The dancing skeletons, the lumbering hunchback buffalos. One day soon it will be the box for you. Give us a story, Lily. Tell us about it. On the street corner spreading her story, all along the countryside, with the Plague Virgin in tow. My story is that I do not want to die. Head banging against the stone wall in the Bargello prison. Please, Please. Foam appearing at the sides of the mouth, the *bubo* a bright beacon of poison.

Lily realizes. My story is the same.

Her mother's trusting face as they hooked up the transfusion.

My story is the same as yours.

Lily's father charting the decline of his baseball team, of all the baseball teams, as his own fortunes slid. No loans available to try again. *Bad risk*. She remembers his face when he said it aloud, said it like he was pronouncing a curious shift in the weather, an upcoming storm that had gone so long unnoticed.

Eppur si muove.

Galileo whispering to the floor tiles as he makes the heavens disappear.

Bad risk. Shrugging, fingering one of his fridge magnets shaped like a falling star.

It does not surprise Lily to see Caterina out under the chestnut tree. She is where she should not be. She appears and disappears like Lily does. She is not from here.

Walk alongside your best friend. Or your executioner. Learn the etiquette and the common sense; Thomas More handing money to the man who will remove his head.

"*Domenica....*", Lily points. "*Santa Domenica.*"

Caterina nods.

Caterina's arm is on Lily's shoulder as they stroll among the trees. Lily can hardly believe that she romped in another clump of trees not long ago, up to her knees in grass, Taddeo's seed on her leg like the petal of a daisy.

She will not hold and love this young body beside her, but she will take the girl's long hair in her hands and braid it as she has braided Beatrice's hair, slowly and formally, as if they had all the time in the world.

The sun is leaving the rooftops. The birds are quiet now, all but a single bird which still sings, its voice the sound of a rusty clothesline cable. Once again Caterina is leading Lily through the streets of the city. They are heading for the Duomo.

Caterina has motioned for Lily to hide in the Duomo, pointing at the doors. But Lily is not prepared to leave Caterina. Caterina is the only one she knows. Whatever happens it will be better with Caterina there.

The tower. Giotto's Tower. The *Lily* Tower!

How come she never noticed — ?

Up the stone staircase, faster, faster. Lily is gasping. The view changes outside the tiny windows as Firenze goes around and around. One level. Another. How high up are they? There is the Duomo. Around, around. There it is again. Yet now she can see the hills beyond the city.

Giotto never lived to see this. His tower existed only in his mind. He dreamed a tower: pink and green and white. Did it disappear when he closed his eyes? Or when he opened them. And is it real now, or only in Lily's mind? Climbing inside, listening for Caterina's footsteps up ahead.

A peaceful darkness descending over the city, coming in from the hills. The trees low with fruit and dew, the boy probably still fishing down by the Arno. Somewhere over there, Michelangelo's *David* gestures at nothing in particular, as a bell sounds for Vigils. Silence is probably something impossible, even here.

Beatrice, my girl, tears are warming my cheeks up here in the night breeze. Beatrice, Mama is on top of the world.

How long they sit and stand and crouch together Lily does not know. She wonders why Caterina does not get it over with. She wonders what weapon Caterina will reveal. Or what signal she will give. Those slight pale hands in the folds of her cloak. The complicity, the ragged complicity of the world.

She hears them on the stairs, clomping up through Giotto's brain, one level and the next. How many have been sent to do the deed? She should be flattered. And what will Caterina be rewarded for her part in all of this? A chair on Church Council?

Caterina is pulling on Lily. Caterina's fingernails, small sharp wedges in Lily's skin. What is she doing? What does she want Lily to do?

"Prego, Lily....Hurry! For God's sake, get over there and stay down!"

Caterina's eyes.

"I'll distract them!"

Three men appear at the doorway. Lily looks up to the invisible constellations. Then a yell.

The man closest to Lily bounds toward Caterina. She is balancing on the edge of the railing. She turns before she leaps.

Lily shrieks.

Caterina's face is now her own.

Caterina flies from the tower, her brown cloak flapping, church bells ringing out around her as she rushes earthward.

Lily shivers at the railing, her hand reaching out to the space that had held the outline.

"Who's this one, then?" she hears a man say.

"Shit, this is great. *We've got her, we think. We're coming out!"*

Caterina on the stones far below, a Japanese print, a slightly larger speck of dust beside the smaller specks of dust. Then Caterina and the tower and all of Firenze disappears.

*

The gear was being ripped from her. Lily shook uncontrollably. Her eyes adjusted to the room. A man and a woman stood over her.

"Good evening, Saint Lily. We've been waiting for you."

Lily rubbed her wrists and squeezed her arms around herself. She eyed her captors coldly. Then she let out a cry. On the floor beside her in the other set of gear lay Bernie.

part 3

Insofar as a humble servant of the faith may respond to and speculate on matters of the faith, I , BURTON N., have compiled an account of the transformation of your servant, LILY DALRIADA. My experience has taught me to view with scepticism early and apparently complete transformations; however, I am offering these findings on the basis of my reputation, confident that both shall be proven worthy.

The subject was defiant upon her entry into the Covenant Centre. While she did not resist her physical removal from the studio of BERNIE DIFIORI, she proved less than cooperative in spirit. It was noted that Lily Dalriada spoke in abusive tones to M. and A. who were transporting her to the Centre. It is also to be noted that her one attempt at physical resistance came as she was being taken from beside the body of BERNIE DIFIORI [whose demise has been listed as a suicide by church and media]. Once removed from the premises of MR. DIFIORI, it was not necessary to apply any restraints to this subject.

Upon entry to the Centre, the subject again made scathing comments, much as an animal strikes with its voice when harnesses prohibit it a physical response.

PROCESSING:

— The subject was stripped and her body washed thoroughly, within and without.

— Photo-Imaging was accomplished and minute imper-fections were removed from the visuals.

— The hips were slightly narrowed in the visuals which, although there is no intention to deny the birth of the Stig child, will minimize reference to it. As well, the breasts were slightly raised in the visuals, to resemble breasts that have not been utilized in the feeding process.

— The subject's hair was shorn.

— The subject then began her training.

QUIET TIME:

LILY DALRIADA entered Cell #7 on the third day of her confinement. She was fitted with spherical translucent glasses that fastened with adhesive to her face. The hair, having been cut short, was no impediment to the eyewear, nor to the MicroWhite Noise filters placed in her ears. These were employed to provide noise nullification while offering as little stimulation as possible. Nourishment was provided in the form of a fortified liquid that could be sipped from a drinking tube by the bed. Urination and defecation were facilitated by a chemical toilet in the corner of the room. The toilet was engineered to be soundless and the chemicals used were odourless.

The subject was instructed to relax and to cease resisting the good graces of the Centre. She was informed that she would remain within the Cell until it was deemed she had completed this stage of her training.

It would be neither productive nor illuminating to note all of the standard responses exhibited by LILY DALRIADA during this period of her training. As in the general number of cases, she began by pacing, shouting, resisting the silence and the unchanging nature of the space. She swore at the monitor behind the window, recited the alphabet, conjugated obscure and arcane verbs. Early on, she slept one twenty-hour period, typical in the first segment of isolation. Awakening, she said she had slept but a half-hour.

Disorientation in time became evident when she was asked indirect time-related questions. Her responses displayed her struggle to keep a fixed time reference, an 'internal clock', in her mind. She commented, for example, that as her hair grew she would know how long she had been "locked up". [This is a classic problem in Quiet Time therapy and not a fault of the method itself.]

Various other responses determined a strong-willed individual in the early stages of training. All of this was to be expected, the Council having chosen LILY DALRIADA presumably because her eventual conversion would convince the Stig population, and the unfaithful, that salvation truly could come to anyone.

After approximately one hundred and four hours in Quiet Time, LILY DALRIADA began experiencing hallucinations. It is my considered opinion that she was hallucinating prior to this period but had maintained her silence in defiance and self-preservation. This is evidenced by the fully-integrated, non-reducible quality of the later hallucinations. After one hundred and four hours, however, the images became so powerful as to cause the subject to respond actively to the hallucinations.

The following list represents the principal documented

hallucinations over a six-hour period:

1) Subject sees a steamroller crushing a flower. The image is repeated until she can focus on a single aspect of the flower — stem, petal, leaf. In one instance, the stem becomes a human arm.

2) Subject smells something she identifies as 'aftershave' in a dark corridor.

3) Subject sees a child falling in a river. This halluc-ination particularly upsets her.

4) Subject sees two people who 'sparkle'. There is music in the background but she cannot identify it.

5) Subject sees a building in flames. The smoke rises in a halo above it.

6) Subject sees a clock. In place of the numbers are small red crosses. In an accompanying kinaesthetic sensa-tion, subject reports feeling herself 'surrounded by feathers'.

7) Subject sees a steamroller crushing a child. This hallucination is somaesthetic and causes such a strong reaction in the subject that she collapses on the floor.

After the monitor entered the room and routine tests determined the subject's condition, a tranquillizer was administered and the subject slept.

THE IMAGE:

Cell #7 was modified to allow the second portion of training to begin. AutoVision apparatus was set up. MicroWhite Noise filters were removed from the subject's ears and she was informed that she would be able to look into the AutoVision box at will. The box opened when a button was pressed. The AutoVision image was fixed and would be changed only at the instigation of the monitor.

The subject resisted for several hours, singing quietly to herself, addressing absent individuals and, at one point, apparently praying.

Her first glimpse into the AutoVision box caused the subject to go silent. The image was that of her daughter, BEATRICE DALRIADA. There was no verbal response recorded throughout this episode.

Two hours later she tried the AutoVision box again. The image had not been altered and, again, there was no verbal response.

It had been determined that the subsequent viewing would involve a different image, along with an accompanying spoken message.

The subject again resisted using the box. It was particularly interesting to note how the isolation eventually wore down this resistance until she was reduced to pressing the button three times in her desperation to view the new image.

THE NEW IMAGE:

The second image was again that of BEATRICE DALRIADA. However, in this instance the child is clearly seen as deceased. The spoken word text is that of Ren Bogen's speech to the newly converted.

LILY DALRIADA has entered the last portion of her training. She is now appearing in person before the faithful. Thus far she is a completely convincing, completely convinced, servant of the Church.

The final phase of her training will occur when she appears before a group of non-believers. We are certain that she will prove herself worthy of the sanctity that is to be bestowed upon her by Church Council. Until that time, we shall continue to study her in all confidence that the wisdom of the Council shall be borne out.

I remain, your servant,

BURTON N.

*

REPORT TO:The Inner Council of the Church of the Survivors
SUBMITTED BY: Maura H., Ecclesiastical Historian

It must first be stated that LILY DALRIADA is the sole live subject who has come before us. We are aware of two earlier live subjects who were processed in the east. However, LILY DALRIADA is the first Stig representative, and as such ours is a significant contribution.

It must here be stated that the function of this department is to provide historical reference and documentation and in most instances this involves third-person research. The bulk of the background research had already been completed when the subject was presented to us. I humbly submit, therefore, first the untouched report written prior to our meeting followed by an account of our meeting with the subject.

> LILY DALRIADA, female, age 38 years
> Born: Temeraire, Quebec, 1972
> Parents: MONA NORRIS, JACK DALRIADA
> Siblings: none

LILY DALRIADA was born to employed, middle-class parents. They moved to Montreal when Lily was a child. JACK DALRAIDA ran a succession of small businesses. His wife, MONA, was a corporate executive. She died in hospital of a transfusion error in 1990. JACK DALRIADA's various businesses failed and when the pre-millennial recession occurred, he retired, eventually moving into a ManorHome where he died in 2002.

LILY DALRIADA showed early signs of unusual sensitivity. An only child, she spent long hours alone talking to herself and her playthings. Extended family (grandparents, uncle) was said to have noted her rich imagination and her ability to enter into otherworldly states that less-subtle observers would have called 'make-believe'.

As a young girl, LILY DALRIADA participated in few group activities. Sports, clubs, and hobbies were encouraged by officials at the school she attended, yet her report cards from this period indicate a child who performed the least possible effort needed to satisfy school participation standards. The one area in which she applied herself appeared to have been the Alchemy Club, a quasi-historical, quasi-scientific school group of little merit. She was forced from this activity when she was required to change schools due to a residential move.

LILY DALRIADA appeared to have been profoundly affected by the premature death of her mother. This single event, which occurred prior to the onset of the Epidemic but which foreshadowed it, hardened the young woman and made spiritual solace, for a time, impossible. The cynicism so rampant in our own age was generated in the seeds of disappointment and unhappiness seen in the young people of this period.

LILY DALRIADA studied for a time at one of the colleges [documents for this period are difficult to locate as it was the beginning of the Restructuring], but, as with so many of her generation, this became a fiscal impossibility. Thus began the young woman's adult employment history.

Aside from summer jobs, LILY DALRIADA had had no employment until the recession necessitated her departure from her studies. [Again, there are no documents as to the nature of her studies.] Her employment history reads as do any number of documents from this period. Following the Restructuring, there were opportunities in the service trade and this is where LILY DALRIADA found work. As a sanitary facilitator, she experienced both the humility so necessary to religious life, as well as the simple satisfaction of a day spent in the service of others. She worked for a time in private homes, for a time in corporations. Her references for this period are impeccable, indicating a conscientious personality already attuning itself to a life of holy service.

Although it would be pleasing as well as fitting to declare the matter closed, it cannot be denied that during this period LILY DALRIADA was engaged in personal encounters with several men. While such incidents were not uncommon at the time, they do establish a pattern that appears to have exerted some control over the woman, leading to the single flaw from which this creature has sought redemption, the intercourse that resulted in the birth of BEATRICE DALRIADA, her natural child, designated "Stig." Her reason muffled by the desires of the flesh, LILY DALRIADA opened herself to a man at the height of the Epidemic and then, still blinded by fear and passion, had documents falsified to state that the child was actually neonatural and approved, thus increasing her culpability.

The Office of Ecclesiastical History wishes to state for the record that it does not believe that children born of these unions are in any way to blame for their unclean parentage. Blameless they enter this world, and it is to the benefit of Church Council that they be brought up to see that it is their parents' error that has caused their societal limitations, not the Church's own strictures.

It has been necessary to describe this unfortunate chapter in order to allow future generations to rejoice in the conversion and eventual redemption of LILY DALRIADA. At the birth of her daughter, LILY DALRIADA entered a most meaningful segment of her existence. She is said to have responded to her daughter exactly as the mother of an approved child would have done. Much of her cynicism dropped away although she retained the wariness that so pervaded the population. This 'happiness', although made possible by illegal documents, appears to have been real enough, the mother and daughter living in an un-quarantined apartment, the mother working to support her child and the child apparently thriving.

When this case was first revealed to us, it seemed a simple matter of moving the mother and child out of the Lister Apartment into a Hansen Block, correcting the falsified documents and informing her employer of the situation. This was done in accordance with our methods.

But when LILY DALRIADA was chosen for sainthood, the most blessed of all honours, she ran in shame from the great event. In her unworthiness she hid herself. This human frailty has enabled her to experience redemption through the Church — this very admission of unworthiness. For is it not through our humbling that we can be lifted up?

I enter this report into the historical record.

Your servant,

MAURA H.

*

ADDENDUM TO REPORT TO: The Inner Council of the Church of the Survivors

SUBMITTED BY: MAURA H., Ecclesiastical Historian

SUBJECT: Personal Interpretation of an Interview with Lily Dalriada

The subject was less than forthcoming during our interview, therefore much of this document necessarily involves my personal interpretation of the encounter.

LILY DALRAIDA was brought before this office following a prolonged session in Cell #7 [*viz.* "Quiet Time" in related documents]. She appeared quite frail, a pale woman with short-cropped brown hair and an expression impossible to read. It is a face that holds mystery, a medieval face. Her body is thin and almost masculine but for the breasts which have suckled a child.

One assumes that the pallor of the skin and the lethargy are at least partly due to her recent isolation experience. A journey out of doors would certainly add colour to the face.

LILY DALRIADA sat in a chair provided for her beside a low table. She was offered refreshment in the form of herbal tisane, or juice, both of which she refused. The historical account was read to her for verification. As has been previously noted, her face betrayed no sign of either approbation or disapproval, but she did shake her head slightly as the conclusion was read. I will quote from this portion of our interview:

MAURA H.: "Is there something you want to add to this? It's *your* history, after all. It will be entered into the record."

[Subject holds the document in the flat of her hand, delicately, as if it is a leaf.]

LILY D.: "The continents are wet...you see...the continents are falling...."

[Subject tips the document which slips from her hand.]

MH: "The...? The story, Lily, is it true?"

LD: "Truth is...light. Truth in the box is ticking. Light is where I go. *Sine sole sileo.*"

MH: "Was your mother's maiden name Norris?"

LD: "The recipe for the little mouse is to plug the telephone cord into the root of the tree."

MH: "There's little point in pursuing this line...."

LD: "Yes, right into the root! Into the root!"

[At this stage the subject became agitated; her face became animated.]

LD: "The continents are falling...the net does not hold."

Her words were strange to the ear, her face suddenly a face of grace and beauty. I thought that it could not be the same woman who had entered the room. She moved to the window and there swayed her hand back and forth in the manner of the willow outside.

The interview was proving most disappointing. There was nothing being revealed that could be entered into the official record. But on the other hand, this office found it most illuminating to see the living breathing woman. So much of the function of this office involves only the historical record. Here was a woman who could be questioned and, no matter how unforthcoming she chose to be, her expressions *did* change. She *heard* me.

I humbly ask that you forgive my next question, for it was a matter of my own curiosity and not the historical record. As LILY DALRIADA stood at the window, I chanced to ask her the whereabouts of her daughter. I was unprepared for the response.

The woman turned to me. Her eyes were terrible. They pierced me, but it was not a look of anger. It was a look of such profound knowledge. Note that I say here knowledge, and not understanding. She did not offer me the gift of her understanding but she *knew* me. I felt that she *knew* me, all of my failings, all of my reasons for asking the question, more reasons that I myself realized. I felt debased, and low. I was *humbled* by this look.

Far be it from me to question the wisdom of Council. I am but a poor servant of the process. Yet my mind was shaken by this woman. I fear we have perhaps erred in pursuing this course. If she is but woman, then have we not wronged this woman in our aspirations for her? But if she is saint — my God, if she is saint — then have we any right at all to be the instrument of her fate?

I submit this personal account with great hesitation. I trust that

Council will bear in mind this office's inexperience in dealing with live subjects. The official record, if it meets with your approval, will stand as such. This account may be dismissed, as may its author, if it will further the aims of your most high Council.

I remain, a faithful servant,

MAURA H.

*

REQUEST TO: The Inner Council of the Church of the Survivors
FROM: ROLAND V.K., Technology/Operations

I am submitting this under protest. It was agreed that my name would not come up in these proceedings. My very livelihood is threatened if this document should fall into the wrong hands, and surely you must realize that it would do your cause no good to have me removed from the strategic position I currently hold.

I am a trusted member of the Underground community. My connections are vast. I ask that you reconsider calling upon me as a witness in these proceedings. I await word.

Yours in the Church,

ROLAND V.K.

*

REQUEST TO: The Inner Council of the Church of the Survivors
FROM: MAURA H., Ecclesiastical Historian

Please be informed that I am having difficulty preparing some of the official documents in the canonization hearing of LILY DALRIADA. My work would be facilitated by a witness statement concerning the role played by BERNIE DIFIORI in this situation. Would Council be so kind as to provide a witness?

Your humble servant,

MAURA H.

*

REPORT TO: The Inner Council of the Church of the Survivors
SUBMITTED BY: ROLAND V.K., Technology/Operations

I arranged to have LILY DALRIADA brought in through the Underground community. They made her welcome and she moved among them. Several community members later stated they believed she was a saint.

I then placed her, temporarily, in a bell tower while arrangements were made to move her elsewhere. I would like to state that due to the inept bungling of one of the other operatives we nearly lost her. The operative also nearly lost his life.

I brought her to the studio of BERNIE DIFIORI. This place was chosen because BERNIE DIFIORI's anti-Church position is clearly known. He has been monitored by church officials for several years. We believed he would make a most credible witness.

LILY DALRIADA was to remain there until such time as Council decided to retrieve her. As BERNIE DIFIORI was to have been a primary witness at the canonization hearings, his unnecessary death — his stupid, heroic death — has been an inconvenience to the Church, making it necessary for me to report to Council in his place.

I feel I am not the right person to make this report. I did not spend time with LILY DALRIADA. I was privy to only a few of her thoughts. I didn't particularly like the woman and, in all honesty, I questioned her choice as Plague Saint. She was too untouched by the disease, too wise to the ways of the world.

I observed her, yes. She greatly loved her daughter, BEATRICE. She also became attached to BERNIE DIFIORI. Most significantly, she showed feeling and concern for the pixel creations she encountered in the *Rebuilt Worlds* program. This is of some appeal, particularly among the downtrodden, but is it enough to justify the sanctity of a woman?

It is my opinion that, had she remained much longer in the company of BERNIE DIFIORI, they would undoubtedly have coupled, which leads me to wonder whether she has learned anything at all from the birth of a Stig child, or from the quarantine in which they have been placed.

BERNIE DIFIORI was a complete failure. Chosen because he defied the Church and, indeed, most authority, chosen because he was a purveyor of virtual alternatives, he apparently 'fell in love' with the saint. How else can one explain why he chose to die for her? I feel I must take responsibility for this failure as the man had come on my specific recommendation.

This experience has caused me to question my ability to read people, a skill which, as you know, is essential in my job. I request, therefore, that I be granted a leave of absence as well as permission to travel between zones. I would like to journey to Québec if passage can be arranged. On the whole, I am exhausted. I wish to travel to a TraveLOG-ON Cabin and watch the maple leaves.

I apologize for the hastiness and informality of this report. I hope

this satisfies your request for information.
Yours in the Church,
ROLAND V.K.

*

REPORT TO:The Inner Council of the Church of the Survivors
SUBMITTED BY: BURTON N., Receptor, Enactor

The subject has responded well to her training. Your concerns regarding her ability to move among the people are, as always, prudent, but I see no reason to prevent the woman from doing what she has been chosen and groomed to do.

My one concern is in the area of her child. As observed in Phase 1 of her training [*viz.* Cell #7 documentation], her response to the images in the AutoVision box was profound. Her attachment to the Stig child is great. The dulling factor seems not to have taken, if the observation of MAURA H., during her interview with LILY DALRIADA, is any indication. The problem, then, is the child. It is my opinion that while this child remains a viable factor in our good saint's life LILY DALRIADA will be unable to give herself fully to the Church.

I recommend the disposal of the child. The mother may then grieve and get on with the good work of the Church.

I PROPOSE:
— Disposing of BEATRICE DALRIADA.
— Informing LILY DALRIADA of her daughter's demise. Documentation   can be provided to aid the completion experience.
— Allowing LILY DALRIADA time to grieve and pray.

Without a child with which to concern herself, and with a life so suddenly empty, I feel confident she will turn to the Church for guidance, for comfort, and for salvation. How much more convincing will her concern for her people be without the distractions of a family?

She may then move among the people freely, and she may then bring truth and honour to her position. And if she contracts and falls to the Disease, she may then become a martyr in the truest sense.

I believe this is the best course of action. I remain,
Your humble servant,
BURTON N.

*

THE PLAGUE SAINT

LILY DALRIADA spoke to people at the North Mall. She came among us with her arms outstretched, like she was open to everyone in the place. She touched hands, even possibly the hands of some people who carry The Disease. She ignored the merchandise and the "Sale" signs, got up on a platform, and spoke. Just talked, but like a person talks when they think they're alone. Thinking out loud, sort of. Gently. Some people seemed nervous at first. The woman I work with said it was creepy, but she was still serving a customer and not really listening.

I was leaning against the glass doors of the shop [*The Game and Glove*]. I was watching it all from there.

This next part is kind of hard to explain. She was planning, I think, to just step down and walk around again in the crowd, when a man shouted something to her. I couldn't hear what. Something that made her bend down on the platform and reach out into the crowd. I couldn't see.

Then, the next thing I know, everyone is crying and blessing themselves and saying things like, "a miracle. A miracle!" I forgot myself and grabbed somebody going by and asked him what was going on. He said that the saint had made a wheelchair man walk.

Everything was very loud and confusing after that. My co-worker told me to close the glass doors because she was afraid of a riot. I started pulling them closed and I felt something, I don't know, something made me turn around. She was looking at me, I swear, she was looking right at me. Her lips were moving but I couldn't hear her. I tried pulling on the doors but they wouldn't budge. Then I heard her voice, but like it was just inside my own ears, my ears alone, and it was saying NO CLOSED DOORS. NO CLOSED GLASS DOORS.

Then...I'm afraid I started crying. I can't explain my actions or my response. I just felt overpowered. Tumbled. I just wanted to leave the store and go off somewhere, walking. I wanted to go walking with this woman and listen to her talk. I stood there, though, with my hand on the door, my co-worker yelling at me to close it. I wasn't able to move.

It was then that the Church official went up to the saint. Nobody heard what he said to her, or what happened to her. She seemed to collapse. The Church official said she was in a religious ecstasy, but she looked sick to me. There was a little girl who was supposed to give the saint some flowers, and the Church official insisted that she hand them to her. She was a little girl with curly hair. The saint looked horrified by her and couldn't hold the flowers, so the Church official took them instead. Then we were told that LILY DALRIADA had spent time working with the quarantined. She was fatigued. She was greatly blessed.

The people went back to the stores and their shopping after that, but some of us...you could tell who because we were kind of looking around at one another...some of us were useless for the rest of the day.

I heard later on the news that she made a final statement while she was at the mall, but I don't remember any statement. I heard that she blessed everybody and offered these words: "The way to a woman's heart is in the breaking of it."

Yours truly,
ANGELA R.

part 4

Chestnut trees and willows washing late colour from the sky. The ground hard beneath her. Winter is underfoot.

Spatiamentum.

The woman walks the lonely white gardens as the monks have done these many years. The clatter of bone-dry branches does not distract her; perhaps she cannot hear them beneath her woollen hood.

Winter. Sparrows clinging to the single branch with berries, clinging or frozen there beneath a curve of ice.

Winter of whistling tunnels of wind. Remember.

But she cannot. A thought, part of a thought, and then nothing. A mind as smooth as the patch of ice ahead, the robe enveloping her, long dark folds to slide her hands into, as if...a bell tolling somewhere. And then nothing.

The child. Child with the golden hair. The child with the lens looking up to the heavens. An icon? She cannot recall. Perhaps from one of the histories.

Whole days it can be like this until the woman tears at her short hair with her fingers. And then will come the seizure of vision, a rupture and the image, the little girl, the little girl, small hand with the flowers disappearing beneath the machine, the flattened body a continent alone on an empty street.

Beatrice.
My daughter.
My daughter....

The woman reaches the end of the garden and turns once again. This time the sparrows on the berry branch are gone.

Words come back like news from far shores, but hollow, hollow in her ear. Sadness pounds, screams into large white rooms that are empty of furniture. The woman has felt the hollow bell, has run her hand around the inside as it hangs. There was a story once, a story or a poem about someone whose lover was due to die when a bell tolled. Unable to bear the thought of losing him, she climbed the bell tower, grabbed hold of the clapper and stopped the clanging with her muffled flesh.

Why this?

Why does she remember this, and not something else? She does not know where she first heard the story. She does not remember that.

In the evenings she hears the chanting of the Vigils, the voices floating down the cold corridors to her cell. In the daytime, from her tiny window, she can just see the hills and a frozen patch of water, a clump of trees and a broken-down, snow- laden fence. A Christmas card from long ago.

In her cot at night she struggles to remember. She has known great sorrow, she feels this is true, and yet there is only kindness, there is peace and kindness. She sees small fish swimming through midnight air, fish and the bottoms of fish. They are swimming in a sea of voices.

Miserere mei, Deus, secundum magnum misericordiam tuam....

The woman listens from beneath the rough wool blanket. The *Miserere?* Someone has died.

In the mornings they rise and say Prime in their cells. Sometimes she wonders how to pray. They all keep to their cells except for the communal services, and there they recite and will not speak to her. There is no one to ask.

There are rooms in the hermitage — there is a corridor no one goes down. The men and women tending the bread ovens and the workshops do not look up from their work, do not seem to notice the wing of the building that abuts the hills. The Abbot, perhaps, has his cell there. For she has never seen him.

She works, as well, sometimes kneading bread with two other monks, sometimes removing snow from the low rooftops with a shovel and a broom. This work is good. She is strengthened by the rhythm and the effort. Returning to her cell, she eats dried fruits, the warm bread. She lies on her cot and closes her eyes but rarely does she sleep.

Figures whirling, the dancing, the joy. Long time ago. Was it a memory? Dancing and laughing. And leaves. Always leaves falling from the golden orange trees.
So many thing that broke the heart.
She does not know why she thinks this.

Do they want her to remember — or to forget? And did that make any difference inside the hermitage? Surely they all had their own memories; they came from some place once.

There are no children here.

And yet she thinks of children, hundreds of children. Perhaps they are all the children she ever knew. She remembers one, a little girl with something smudged on her hands. Pink ink. Something. A picture of a boy and on the top of the picture the words: *Nick of Time*. Another stamp on the other hand, an old man leaning on a cane, his curved body like one half of a heart. And above him, too, the words: *Nick of Time*. The little girl laughs at the pictures and claps her hands together.

That was me.
The girl missing a front tooth.
That was me.

The woman rises from her bed. She will join the community for Vespers. She adjusts her robe and then looks down at her hands, at the calluses from the snow shovel. She presses her hands together slowly, almost as if she were praying.

*

The snow has isolated the grey hermitage on the hill. Contact with the outside world, always minimal, has ceased. The monks perform their labours and sing praises and the days pass seamlessly.

The woman has become adept at bread-baking and at knitting scarves and socks which are distributed among the members of the faithful. The wool is slush-coloured, like a Persian lamb coat she remembers seeing as a child.

Yes, she remembers now, some things anyway. She cried out at night the first time she saw her parents' faces in the dark and then allowed herself to drift with their images as far as they would take her. Her mother's hands, happy in the flowerbed, now manicured and clammy on the way to the office meeting. Sometimes her mother travelling down the elevator, all the numbers falling, to step out in the lobby and walk toward her daughter.

How proud the girl had felt when her mother spoke to her there, people turning to see this busy woman checking a child's homework over on the bench. The pictures always flashed brightest as she watched her mother in the hospital, smiling weakly and waving from behind the glass.

It flashed and went out and the woman lay in the blackness and remembered at last.

They put her behind the glass while she was still alive.

They put her in a *lazaretto*!

The daughter's fingers pressed up to the pane. Molecules and atoms and infinity between.

Galileo's atomism.

A mother's fingers shifting slightly off the sheet.

That was my goodbye.

Tears in the blackness as the Vigils are sung to the stars.

*

What day is it, what date? Winter, but winter is a long time in this country. She feels the need to know which small square on the calendar she can claim. But there are no calendars here; she has not seen one since she arrived. What use is a calendar in this order? Here no one ever leaves, or writes or teaches. Here the doctrine is not discussed or debated or even praised. Here you work and pray, mostly, in silence, and then one month, one year, it doesn't matter which year, you fall in the meadow after tending the apple trees and you are brought in on a litter; a funeral mass is sung and you are buried in the graveyard with no headstone and no marker.

She has seen one such funeral.

The man's name was not mentioned except once during the service, and the brother departed the earth anonymously. No wise lessons, no attributable teachings. Around here you came and went and no one even noted what day it was.

September 23.

September 23, the child was born.

She rolls this thought over and over.

*

It is an ordinary day, a day perfect in its sameness. The woman is clearing snow from the doorway to the central chapel. She sweeps along the walkway listening to the wind whipping the cloister. She is suddenly, so suddenly, before it that she stops cold and stares at the

RITA DONOVAN

heavy wooden door.

Through there is the far wing, the closed section of the hermitage. She begins swishing the snow around the door stoop although no one uses this door.

The ease with which it budges surprises her. She leans her tools up against the wall, removes her wool mittens and pushes with both hands. A wedge of snow hits the floor as the door yawns open.

Bare hallways, sienna tiles, small leaded windows frosted with gritty snow. The light is translucent, the corridor as ice cold as those in the drawings of the Snow Queen's palace.

Yes, she remembers that, too.

The Abbot's cell?

A private chapel?

An office, the kind of stuffed leather chairs no longer permitted to be made, a long wooden desk, probably oak. She remembers polishing furniture like this, the full sweep of the cloth, the glow a hundred layers down. A cabinet of books, some very old. The glass door to the shelf is locked.

She wonders if she can talk to someone here. An office like this with its inviting chairs would be used for meetings and consultations.

So, what was it doing in the hermitage? Holdover from the glory days of a rich denomination? The furniture in the cells was hand-hewn and simple. No such thing as an oak desk the likes of which had disappeared at the millennium.

Computer link-up. To whom? To what?

She sits down at the terminal and turns it on.

Okay, that was simple enough.

The emblem of the Church of the Survivors appears on the screen, a dove on the shoulder of a sexless stick-figure. She has always found the emblem silly, and the stick figure is so neutered it makes the figure at the cross-walk look pornographic.

The emblem disappears and the terminal automatically begins scrolling the latest Church news. There are three more churches opening across the country, the hugest in the Sky Dome where they used to play ball.

She is about to experiment with the keys when something, some instinct she barely recognizes, kicks in. She shuts down the terminal and repositions the chair at the desk.

Nothing. Nowhere.

Then she sees the low window ledge and the heavy brocade curtains. Quickly, lifting her robe as she bolts, she is up on the ledge and behind the curtain. The air is freezing so close to the window. She sits as far to the side as she can, draws in her breath and presses her head against her knees.

The Abbot enters the office and sits down at the desk. He is in his late sixties, easily, with a tonsure of grey. He seems lost in thought, mulling something over as he presses his fingertips together. She bites her knee and lets the pain refocus her. Already the cold is cramping her legs. His face turns her way. Lily lets out a silent shriek. She is staring at Ren Bogen. She can see why they never photographed him in straight-on portrait. His eyes. His eyes are so wide and empty, dark like the drop beneath the gallows.

He seems comfortable enough, pulling on the end of his nose as he mutters. There is a knock at the door and he grunts. The door opens to reveal a man whom she remembers as the one who comes to choir only occasionally. She has thought that he must be ill since his comings and goings have been so erratic. He is a short slight man with a constant cough and a mouth that he is always covering. This habit, and the cough, and a naturally thin voice has guaranteed that he has not been missed singing the mass, but also makes it difficult to determine what he is saying from across the room.

He speaks with Ren Bogen and together they call up something on the screen. Papers are signed, the monk coughs some more, and nods as he points at the screen.

"These are fine reports. You've done good work, brother."

The short man acknowledges with something between a nod and a grimace as the little hand comes up to the mouth again, an early sign of the Disease? Certainly, the fear of the Disease.

"Have you discovered anything else about the child?"

She is rigid with attention.

The short man taps his nose with the flat of his hand as if taming a sneeze.

"We have the guardian but have been unable to persuade her to cooperate."

Now it is Ren Bogen who mutters, something about inconvenience, a great inconvenience.

"She must not learn of this. If she were to know that the child...well, you understand."

The little man nods vigorously. He makes another short bow and leaves the room.

Ren Bogen shakes his head then returns to the documents on his desk. He sits very still. What is he doing? She watches as the man closes his eyes and prays.

Lips moving. No words, no sound.

The child. Can it be?

She squeezes herself into a ball behind the curtain, squeezing her body warmth in upon itself, hugging one thought above all others: can it be?

As he prays, she remembers the rubber-stamp order her father had fulfilled for the Christian Summer Camp, and the stamps she had played with, flowers and butterflies and in bold letters: *Say One For Me!*

Look at this man! The bent posture of a scholar, the unhealthy face, eyes that seem to move back and forth even when they are closed. This is the Voice of the Church of the Survivors. Father of all Creeders. Scratching his nose.

Her toes are frozen.

Ren Bogen has fallen asleep.

The sunlight is lower on the translucent pane.

Lily steals around the furniture and out of the room.

*

The woman remembers being let out of this place to minister to the sick, to move among the coughing wheezing beds. Men and women, even small children, share these green walls, the clang-clang of the metal cart going down the hall.

She has spoken very little since arriving, preferring to glide from bed to bed touching a forehead here, a hand there. Fingers reach after her as she departs the lonely island of each bed, mouths bless or ask for blessing.

Beside some beds are seated Buddhas. Over some beds are crucifixes. Above still others, Elvises. Anything is allowed here. This is where they come to die.

Lazaretto, she thinks, and can see again the coined faces, the marble chapels and the wax bodies hanging in the cathedral candlelight. A lone litter carried up the hillside to the *lazaretto*. The perfect city breathing below.

One woman more lucid than the others grasps the saint's hand, have mercy, please, please, look — look at my palm! — what does my palm say? As the other hand makes the sign of the cross in jerking rhythm.

Sometimes it is so cold in these rooms that the staff wear mittens over their protective gloves, which is jarring with the surgical masks. No one touches these people, not directly. No one but her.

Some are clearly infected and her touch is light on their burning foreheads. Others look healthy enough but are simply too weary to rise up from their beds. She sees this, both their exhaustion and their quiet resignation. Their hands clasp ever more weakly. For some it is all fear and anguish. And she nods and whispers, "We arrive in tears, we depart in tears, and in between the possibility of *so much* joy."

Old gentlemen clinging to pillows when they once clung to their wives.

And the children.

The little boy with scars across his face. A face only a mother could love. And she understands. Understands it all and embraces the spare body with its small bones. The boy whose mother had fallen at work, had been brought here wearing the mark of contagion, the boy wild in the halls, sneaking in to pull the face mask down. "I want to see my Mama smile."

The saintly woman rocks the little torso, humming a song she remembers from a thousand years ago.

Oh, Beatrice.

The fingers brush along his arm like a spider.

Afterwards, she sometimes sits in the common room with the food machines. The room is off-limits to all patients, but her presence is tolerated although she is left to herself.

She hears whisperings all around her, like leaves overhead on a cool autumn night, chattering just before they fall. Secrets. Secrets. The doomed or the damned, she does not know which, but names dart past her ears, this one who bribed an orderly and went home to die, that one who walked out of the ward and lay down in front of the screaming ambulance. Stories of people who simply walked away with their names and identities and disappeared.

She watches the talker swill his machine soup.

Back at the hermitage she paces her cell as faces appear one after another. The boy who followed his mother into the morgue. The man who had smiled — yes, smiled at her from his emaciated face which even then she remembered as that of the hotel clerk who had hidden her once.

"I'm so glad you came," he said softly, holding her hand. "I am honoured by your presence. Please pray for me. And for the little one."

She can hear the bell calling them to service yet she remains in her cell, turning over faces and words.

Pray for me. *And for the little one.*

At the time, another child's limp body had filled her arms and thoughts. Now she hears in the loud clap of the bell the words —

If the child were...if her daughter were still alive....

— and the pain of such hope bends her double. And then she is kneeling, praying and crying and laughing at the thought.

The bell ceases and the voices begin chanting and she is still on her knees, her head pressed to the floor, like Galileo looking up diagonally at the power of the Church, muttering a curse to the stones.

Eppur si muove!

Yet, it moves!

Galileo's ladder over his tomb, a marble road out of the sarcophagus.

To the stars, he points.

Through the window there are stars!

*

In the small rooms of houses where they dream and toss their heads, she bathes sick bodies, and the bodies tell her many things. Scars from encounters with plate-glass windows, the legs ribboned like the Bizarro Superman in the old comic books. Heads with scars at the carotid artery, stomachs with the reminders of caesarians and laparoscopies. Cauterized stains on the neck and the shoulders, tendons slit and straightened, slit and straightened.

And the others, the burn scars, small dollops of great pain doled out over a decade, children with welts that always end just at the edges of their sleeves.

THE PLAGUE SAINT   137

In the small rooms they dream and pray. They show her everything. It is a relief to lift this burden. It is a blessing to share this rough gravel road. There is good silence, too, in washing the body after death. Silence that allows more dignity than the previous year or years have allowed. Silence that swallows the old woman on the bed and says with every breath she does not take: *I am more than the sum of my parts.*

And back in the hermitage when the Vigils have been sung and all is quiet, the saint wrestles with these words that sound like something she would read on a rubber stamp, struggles and yet the words do not go away, and do not break down, any more than the faces of the bodies go away. Anymore than the thought of the child goes away.

I believe she lives.

She sends the words up to the ceiling. Outside the stars move around the hermitage, a splendid carousel.

I choose to believe?

She rises from her bed and puts on long grey knitted stockings. Her robe falls over her nightshirt.

I believe. I believe she lives.

*

Uncle Philly tugging on her seersucker jacket. "Come with me, Chodio-Babe, come with me!" And taking her to the top of the mountain to overlook the city. "Up here you see it all."

Peering through the rental magnifying lens.

"Topless," he grins, the steel eyes aimed at an apartment rooftop.

"Or here," and swings the device around to press up against the flat ribbon of the St. Lawrence River. "It's just like licking a map! You're so close, so...you can *feel* the shine on that water!"

Uncle Philly obviously amplifying his senses with something.

She smiles at him, always looking for the shiniest bit of paper. He is a little like her, or rather she like him, except she feels so much older than this uncle who leaps, now, around the lookout like a madman, who sits stone-still, a gargoyle on the ledge.

"Don't...Uncle Philly, come down!"

The smile as wide as the jawline will permit because she has given him his line once again.

"Never come down, Babe. I never come down."

Below the giant blinking crucifix they sit, two people linked by blood. His blood so like his sister's, her mother's. His blood that might have saved her. Or so he believed. And believed and believed. A life balanced so precariously on uneven stones, so easy to topple onto the flat plain of the picture.

It would be nice to remember him happy. To remember all of them happy and thriving and deep in the midst of the small family turbulences that become the tracking mechanism of memory.

"You see it all up here, Babe."

Uncle Philly's broken canine when he smiled.

*

The silence of the cloister is frightening. She would welcome the tubercular coughs of the old brother with the limp. The corridor, all of the corridors, are deserted, including the one leading to Ren Bogen's study.

When she cleaned offices she would enter empty rooms like this, witness the day's mess of trade and enterprise and clear debris from desks and garbage pails.

This room is spotless.

The wood gleams. The lamp glows warmly. Like her grandfather's study in the old house in the country, inviting yet private, like her grandfather himself.

Where to begin? She scans the file list beneath the top flap of the desk blotter, something she had learned from years of cleaning offices. The key file names were always jotted there, or on the bottom of coasters, or on the edges of calendars.

Her finger runs down the list. One title leaps at her:

LILY. ST.

"Roll 'em", her father's command, and Lily flicking off the living room light, the old film galloping onto the scene in "glorious black and white". Lily's father blowing pretend smoke into his hands and then releasing it in an imaginary puff that told her it was magic.

In another room — another time? — Beatrice on the floor hooting at the antics of the cartoon mice, strutting bow-legged into the saloon, the original Sheriff Galileo.

She catches her breath.

This.

This body, this woman among the sick. This is not her. A face that she no longer has claim to — legal rights on faces now as fuzzy a picture as the background trees in old movies. A tallness, a kind of tallness or thinness she does not recognize. Eyes so sure, so blank with purity, open to only one kind of wonder, the one emanating from her own whispers and fears.

The hands aren't mine.

Placed on the head of the dying plague victim.

Why didn't they use her hands?

She looks down at her hands, turns them over, watches the fingers press the keys that will take her deeper into the file.

The saint is seen among the Stigs. They are hailing her as one of their own. Stig children run this way and that and, as they do, she searches the screen intently.

There is a Hansen Block, although it is not her own.

There are the faces of the forlorn.

There is the saint gliding through the building, her robe touching each side of the narrow dim hallway.

The saint removes her robe to place on the bed of a blue-veined child and stands in her thin shift. It is evident that the breasts, too, have been altered.

Further, further into the file.

Show me what else you have done in my name. With my face. Without my hands.

He is behind her before she knows it.

"Roland!" she hisses. "Are you crazy? What are you doing here?"

He stands over her, his eye on the terminal.

"That was the question I had for you. I see you've been catching up on the news. I've tried to keep things simple for you, but you insist on muddying the waters."

"You? What do you mean?"

He takes his hands off the desk. Two imprints remain. He paces now.

"Look...it isn't my idea to be here. I'd just as soon be skiing. In fact, I was called back for this. So I'll make it quick. You aren't adapting as well as we'd hoped. The Quiet Time seems to have altered you but it hasn't transformed you and that has been disappointing to us."

"Us? To *us*?"

He glares at her.

RITA DONOVAN

"Look, don't sit there and judge me."

She can't believe it.

"The last time I checked you weren't God yet! Sure, I work with the Church. I keep an eye on things in the regions, okay? I keep a *lid* on things. And before you start with that, you think back to the panic when the Disease first hit. Remember? Sheer utter fucking panic. The thirty people on the bus driven over the canyon cliff like they were buffalo? Or that news reporter who killed herself on the air because she was afraid she had it?

"Insane. Everything falling apart all around us. Right? You and me and everybody else terrified and suspicious and dangerous. Yeah, dangerous. And I told myself then and there I would do whatever it took to contain this thing. If I was a smoke-jumper you'd be cheering me on!"

"Roland — "

"No! I don't want to hear it! Yes, I infiltrated the underground groups. Yes, I have lied my way into privileged positions but — and my documents will support this — I have personally diffused situations that would have led to panic and more death in Toronto, in Montreal, in Vancouver. And even here. So before you sit there and *judge* me — "

"Roland," Lily closes her eyes. Her head is brimming. Rubber stamps with messages she cannot read keep appearing, falling forward over the edge of a metal table. "Listen," she says quietly. "We still have the Disease...and we're still terrified, and suspicious. We are still dangerous."

Roland crosses his arms. The querulous expression appears for just a moment before he adjusts his face.

"Lily Dalriada, I have been instructed to reveal certain things to you, to offer you some knowledge, if you will. Some of this will not be pleasant. I wish you had left well enough...God, I wish I were skiing....but — "

He pushes Lily's chair toward the large oak wardrobe.

" — that is not the case."

He opens it and Lily recognizes the equipment. All at once she sees Caterina at the bottom of the Lily Tower, Bernie on the floor of the studio.

"No No, I won't go back inside! No! It's not real!"

"It is *all* real, Lily. *All of this!*"

He waves his hand skyward.

"This hermitage. *Real* monks, *real* prayers. Or, it is nothing. Just like it is in there. Take your choice. That's what makes it so tough, Lily. That's why some of us have a *tough time* with our consciences."

"I won't go back inside."

"Lily, how do you know you aren't in there already?"

She kicks and struggles as he tries to take off her clothes.

"Stop it, Lily! Don't you want to see what happens?"

"You're crazy!"

"No. No, I'm not. But you are one of the few people who is being offered a choice. Think of how many out there, how many sick or hopeless people, wished they had any choice at all!"

Lily stands still. She is outfitted.

"I like your breasts better. But I like her hands. They were designed after the hands of the medieval St. Christina the Astonishing.

"Listen. Listen to me. The Church feels you've done a good job with the victims, and you're being claimed as a Stig saint *by* the Stigs. The Church feels your time here is limited. They don't want anything to ruin the good work you've done. But you're curious. You just happen to be one of those nosy saints. So, here, they're saying. You want knowledge? Here is knowledge."

*

Rags and splendour, encrusted goblets with shiny half-moons of wine tipped up to her lips and then taken away. Arms...her hands. Her hands in irons. These people, these men in robes so heavy, so dark.

Are they real?

Are the pincers real?

Are these breasts that look like her breasts as real as — as hot — hot —

A scream.

Silence. Ceiling.

Buffalo and naked children driven over the cliff, the black buffalo dragging the Triumph of Death, straining against the wagon-load of bones.

Blood flows from her nipple like milk, like a stigma. She tries to raise her hand but it is held fast and...she sees now, it is not her hand at all.

The pain, she thinks.

The pain is mine.

I am more than the sum of my parts, she prays.

The Tower is not Giotto's. Lily swaying. No air. No light. Just a dismal pocket of agony. Just a pattern in space.

"I don't believe in you," she whispers through dry lips.

The man takes down her testimony.

"A non-believer!" he nods.

There is the rack. Or the rope. Or the breaking on the wheel. Crushed by a door, O Margaret Clitherow. A knife to the throat, O Lucy of Syracuse.

"Someone will know," she murmurs.

"Really? Who will know? Who do you represent, Lily Dalriada?"

She struggles for words.

"They killed...Jan Nebomuk... but the stars...the stars told what they did."

The candlelit ceiling, and then all is dark.

*

"Lily...."

Roland's hand on her shoulder.

She jumps and fights him, her arms free but for the equipment.

"Lily, it's okay. Look. Here. We're here."

She lashes her arms across her breasts and gasps for breath.

"Listen, Lily..."

"I don't believe it. Do you hear me!"

Roland wheels around.

"And do you think they believe in you? Who are you anyway? Some cleaning woman. Some goddamn night cleaner elevated to the position of SAINT! For the good of the people out there who need something, anything, to hang on to. Who the hell do you think you are! Well, never mind. We're not finished. We're talking options here. Vision. Knowledge. You want to see God, Lily Dalriada? You want to know what all the dominoes look like?"

He thrusts her back into the headgear. She thrashes and then it appears.

*

Perfect.

THE PLAGUE SAINT   143

How could they know this? How could they know the stain on the table, the paint chip missing on the end? The ugly walls, too, are absolutely right. Hansen Block M-D4.

Beatrice's drawing on the refrigerator door. A girl with a big blue hat, her fist enclosing a riot of colour. Wildflowers. Lily remembers. Beatrice had not drawn "their bodies" because, she said, they were still moving.

She is mad with the hope that she will see —
"Beatrice?"
Her own voice thunders in her ears.
"Bea?"
She tries to walk through the door leading to Beatrice's bedroom but the space, although appearing open, is impossible to enter. She can see down the hall, a set image that tracks when she moves her head, but if she tries to step through it the picture disappears and there is only a grid.
"Where are you, Bea? Where is she?"
The calendar on the wall is at least two months behind. It is snowing at the hermitage but here it is autumn.

*

This time when Roland removes her she is silent and unmoving. Roland opens the credenza and pours Lily a chalice of wine. White gold, a thin band of amethysts and a cross shaped of rubies.
"Who did this belong to? The previous tenants?"
"They don't need it anymore. Go ahead."
She sips the sweet wine. "Mass wine."
"Or whatever he can get his hands on. Look, I'm trying to help you, Lily."
"Then find Beatrice."
"Beatrice. Lily, you know, you were told about her death."
"Bea is not dead."
"You can't believe...."
She grabs Roland's arm. "She isn't dead! You know it!"
He shakes the wine from his sleeve and sighs.
"I didn't want to have to do this. Despite what I've told the Church, I don't, in fact, dislike you, Lily. I just wish you liked yourself a little more and would spare yourself the misery."

*

When her eyes become accustomed to the dark she realizes it is the little church in Firenze, the Portinari church. There is Mona Tessa's sarcophagus. Candlelight sparks across the stone features.

Her eye is drawn, against her will, to the small draped box before the altar. She cannot prevent herself from stepping toward it even as she is looking away.

No.

The lace-work around the pillow. A peace much quieter than sleep.

"No! I don't believe it!"

She smashes her hand against her eyes and when she opens them the image has changed. Now she sees the outside of a series of Hansen Blocks. It is a slow pan shot, like the shot of Citizen Kane's belongings, like the cowboys looking out across the Red River or the Shenandoah Valley.

— *See that, Lily? See the economy of movement there?*

Her father's glee at a perfect use of landscape. Another classic film for the collection.

She sees now that it is a slow pan shot up the driveway of Hansen Block M-D4.

The hallways are silent.

"You want me to believe they're all dead? Okay! Everybody died of the Disease. Next!"

The doorway to her apartment opens on its own. The furniture has been piled in the center of the room. Citizen Kane again. Savonarola.

"Rosebud!" she yells. Her daughter's chair, her daughter's copybooks, amateur telescope balancing on top.

"Wrong!"

When she shakes her head the image tracks left and right. She backs from the room and tries to continue down the hall but once she gets to the end she cannot open the door to the stairwell.

"No upstairs...and no Anna and no Giulia...and NO DEATH!"

*

Roland pulls the headgear from her, staring into her disoriented face. She rocks back and forth and then is still. She focuses on his face.

"Beatrice is alive, Roland. For all I know, Bernie is, too."

"Would you care to see his putrid corpse?" Roland snaps. "It can be arranged."

"Like everything?"

The moon is bright on this cold cold night. Roland throws her robe at her.

"They want you finished."

"So why don't they finish me?"

He shifts his gaze to the icy window. "I've tried to convince them it isn't in their best interest. They really don't want to go into the relic business. And, after all, people *will* want to see the body. Even with the best presentation and preservation techniques, it's hard to take that on the road anymore, which is what they'd have to do because of the quarantine. It's not like it was with Lenin. It's not a pilgrimage."

Lily's heart feels swollen. She holds her hand across it and presses. Is it possible...?

"But you keep mouthing off about Beatrice, about her being alive, and you keep going on about that pathetic Difiori. It isn't good for the Church. It raises questions, gets people talking. Well, they say, if this isn't real then what am I doing living like hell?"

"So, what are they doing living like hell?"

"*See? That* has to stop! That's what they're afraid of. They tried with the Quiet Time; they tried to show you."

She does not hear him. She is thinking of Beatrice, of finding Beatrice and walking away from this world, a world built on consensus after all.

"Lily...if you were silent...if you went into a cloister."

"I'm *in* a cloister!"

"I mean really. Into a cave or something."

"You found me in a cave, remember?" She speaks softly, for she sees in him some private anguish for all of this. "I'm still in a cave, Roland. "Maybe you are, too."

"One, okay...one more. Once more." He grapples with the gear. "This isn't one of theirs. I found this myself in an obscure maintenance program. AUDIE EX. He must have known, don't you see, and done it before he died. Look...listen. All of this is possible."

*

She is in a bedroom. A red damask coverlet is draped across the bed. She sits down on the edge and fingers the rich cloth. A mobile sways overhead. It is the fish. The shadows play on the ceiling just as they always have, and when he enters it is only a little surprise.

"Hah!"

A low bow. A blue-jay pelt smoking jacket.

"I am honoured by your telepresence," he says.

Lily is biting her lip.

"If you found me it means you've gotten over your disdain for the machine. And it also means I am probably dead."

She is afraid to speak. Is this just a monologue on a loop? Can she interact with him?

"Bernie...."

A smile. Recognition. Caterina's eyes in his stubbled face.

Her own eyes fill. "Thank you...." She cannot go on. "Thank you for giving your life — "

The words. She is insane.

"Lily...may I call you Saint Lily? If you're here listening to me it means you are still among the mortals. I'm sorry I wasn't more of a help. I wanted to ride away with you into the sunset, you know, a man, his horse, his saint — "

"Bernie."

The voice stops. A slight smile plays on his face.

She is afraid to talk. How much could he have programmed? She is afraid to say the thing that will make him disappear into the patterned grid. "I don't know what to say."

"Come on, in the perfect film, or rather, in my perfect film, we don't spend all our time talking," he grins.

She swears she can smell his awful cologne even as she is climbing the pillows and brushing up against his jacket.

She is kissing and laughing at the same time as Bernie catalogues all of the body parts he has digitally improved.

"Patented...you know that? This one is patented. Haptic magic," he swoons. His hands encircle her breasts as if they are moulding clay and he is laughing, too, at the inspired clumsiness, the artful absurdity, of this passion.

"Brando's," he huffs, inflating his chest.

"What?" she manages.

"Brando's chest!"

They both glance at the muscles working.

"You know...before."

"Before!" she repeats and they explode in laughter, Brando's chest and Bernie's mind and Galileo's finger.

He lies beside her and traces her hand along his stomach.

"I removed the appendix scar," he explains. "Who needs the appendix and who needs the scar?"

Lily covers their bodies with the damask bedspread.

"Shame?"

"Are you kidding? We never looked so good."

"Go ahead, say something about perfect," he says softly.

"Well, we're certainly a conglomeration of all the egocentric bastard — "

"Just say it."

"Oh, Bernie, oh, baby, you were perfect."

"I didn't mean me. But it'll do."

And into the room walks a small girl in a quilted robe.

Beatrice giggles and races to join them on the bed. From under his pillow Bernie takes a yo-yo and winds the string around his finger. He smiles at Lily, sits up and flicks his wrist. They all watch the red spinning yo-yo travel out the length of the string. As it reaches its limit a window appears on the far wall. From the window Lily can see the dusty sienna rooftops of Firenze.

Bernie starts humming an old tune.

"*I've got the world on a string.*"

He shrugs.

"And it fits in my pocket."

His arm on Lily's shoulder, and Beatrice asleep between them, her breathing light against Lily's arm.

The golden dome of her head.

"Where are we?" Lily whispers.

He leans over above Beatrice and kisses Lily's forehead.

"We're here. We're together. Always."

*

The tiles are freezing under her feet despite the heavy woollen socks. Roland takes her wordlessly back to her cell. Moonlight through all the frozen windows. Winter stars.

She remembers now. She remembers everything.

part 5

REPORT TO:The Inner Council of the Church of the Survivors
SUBMITTED BY: ROLAND V.K., Technology/Operations
SUBJECT: SAINT LILY DALRIADA

In what I trust will be my final report on this matter, I am entering into the record information concerning the former LILY DALRIADA.

Following her training, repentance and alteration, the former LILY DALRIADA, henceforth referred to as originating human STELLA LASCAUX, performed admirably among the sick and dying.

In what I perceive to have been a misjudgment on Council's part, the woman was then informed of the death of her child [Stig child BEATRICE DALRIADA], a move calculated to draw her completely within the folds of the Church. The woman denied her daughter's death and the weave of realities, so carefully constructed, began to shred around her. Her questions were, and are, of the nature that could damage the credibility of the Church of the Survivors and cause chaos if allowed to spread.

While her digitalized self continued to inspire and comfort her followers, the originating human grew more agitated within her confinement. Having no guarantee that, at the time of her proposed death, she would in fact "go gentle into that good night", there remained two possibilities: finish her quietly and unexpectedly, which would leave the problem of her body, relics and the inevitable unauthorized pilgrimages, or continue with SAINT LILY DALRIADA, *without the encumbrance of the originating human.*

When this latter proposal was presented to her, she agreed to depart the person of LILY DALRIADA. She agreed to all the conditions regarding the transfer of persona:

— that she would undergo surgery to alter her facial appearance in keeping with the Church's proprietary rights on LILY DALRIADA's digital image.

— that she would relinquish her name and all custodial rights to her name, taking a new name of her choosing, in this case, LASCAUX.

— that given the extraordinary circumstances of her case, and the danger of discontent and disbelief in the event of any preaching she might desire to do, she would undergo the surgical removal of her tongue.

These conditions were agreed upon and were enacted under my supervision. Following her recovery, STELLA LASCAUX was provided with a package of food, the same provision the Church makes for any of its faithful. She was then released. She has disappeared and I trust she will not be heard from again.

SAINT LILY DALRIADA spoke on television recently, calling for tolerance and compassion for the many homeless people wandering the countryside, but it is my opinion that given the heavy quarantines in the cities, wanderers will not be well-treated.

With this conclusion, I request a leave of absence from church-related duties. This case has been protracted and difficult and, while I am secure that it has concluded satisfactorily, I must confess to certain misgivings involving the originating human.

Council should please note my general fatigue and consider it a factor in this request.

I remain,

Yours in the Church,

ROLAND V.K.

*

They were her hands. All the years of watching them work, stacking and polishing, picking up after Beatrice. Covered in stamp-pad ink and rolling joints for Uncle Philly. They were her own hands.

She lifted and flung the small bag across her back and fixed the strap upon her shoulder. They had opened the doors and she had stepped out into a budding earth-scented world. Springtime, and while the birds chirped furtively, they did sound the season and she had almost opened her mouth to sing with them before feeling, again, the absent tongue. Still, she felt such fullness. Her heart hurt and she pressed the heel of her hand to it.

The heavy socks and sandals would soon be wet. She would find an outlet that dispensed the clothing of the dead. Such places were not permitted and yet they existed, *rigattieri*, and had always existed. Like she, too, existed.

She began walking. The roads, the back roads, were not watched as they should be. It would take her longer to get home, but then she had nothing but time. She wished, though, that she owned a map. All those years reading star charts and maps in dimly-lit offices.

They told her that her daughter was dead. Besides, they reminded her that even if the child was alive she wouldn't know her mother. The child would see her mother on the news and hold her hand up to the screen. The child would have someone else who tucked her into bed, who smoothed the hair back from her face. The child would not know her.

Stella Lascaux allowed herself occasional moments of anguish. The first came when she saw her reflection in the long steel medical cabinet after the bandages came off.

What had she expected? Gloria Swanson's frozen Norma Desmond from *Sunset Boulevard*? The head-shaped air beneath Claude Rains' bandages in *The Invisible Man*?

A face. Not hideous, not unpleasant. Not hers.

Her face, her mother's and father's DNA disco dance, belonged to a saintly woman who moved among the bodies of the sick. Who never smiled. And if she did smile, whose teeth would she reveal?

The thought made her smile and her hand went up to the strange new mouth and felt the chip in her front tooth. Her tongue used to do that, absent-mindedly poke at the slightly-jagged tooth.

She allowed the anguish when she thought of her voice. Not a special or significant voice. One that carried a tune, she remembered; one that comforted Beatrice when she cried in the night. Now it brayed. Now she was a eunuch in the harem. Or Pinocchio morphed into a donkey.

Galileo lost his finger.

Domenica da Paradiso lost her ears.

Lily's tongue, now, in a bottle of formaldehyde. Or freeze-dried. To be reunited someday in Heaven?   Galileo's finger pointing and all of these pieces knocking at the Gates of Paradise, Ghiberti's gates, looking for their owners.   Who aren't their owners after all.

She had given it all away. And yet, she felt somehow herself. She had given it all away except Beatrice.

Standing in the Church of Santa Maria Novella, marvelling at the round high windows projecting circles onto the walls. Voices rise, lilting, just as a bird flies by outside. The shadow of the bird moves across the round bright circles. She reaches her hand up, but neither are there. The bird disappears into the creviced wall.

Beatrice, my Beatrice, I will find you. We are not fooled by appearances, you and I. Mama has changed and you will change, too.

Your hair might go auburn like your Grandma's. And your teeth will come out and you'll put them under your pillow and you will also believe.

As I believe.

*

They had offered her the world. Beatrice, and Bernie, Florence on the end of a string, a Firenze without plague if she wished, or a TraveLOG-ON Florence teeming with people, tiny cars like baby booties, motorbikes like insects crawling over the stones.

A world so mutable, after all.

Or a choice, at last, to be where she was.

*

She came upon two men on the road. One hobbled even as the other supported him. She thought that they were not going to glance up, so carefully were they watching the uneven gravel road, but then as they were only yards from her they looked up, both of them. The lame one smiled.

Lily took down her pack and opened the drawstring. There were things here she could no longer eat. Thick crusts of monastery bread. Some ripened cheese.

"Bless you!" they nodded and then tore into the food, eating where they stood, hunched over like dogs choking down large chunks of meat.

*

She walked along.

She could understand now how cathedrals were built over centuries, each labourer securing his stones, swinging higher up the scaffolding, talking only to the silent stones. And waking up each day enfolded in his vision, carving his initials in the place where he would die.

This is where I am, he whispers to the stones, loving pink and white and green in his cool hands. And if he hears the swallows from the non-existent bell tower, or the bells of other churches around him at this height, the sounds live on in this one moment, the moment when he knows that he is here.

Here, beloved of the stones.

She smiled at this, and felt the earth loosen beneath her sandals. Bea's head bobbing up and down as the girl hopped to her stone and

RITA DONOVAN

picked it up. One foot, two feet, one foot, HOME. Yes.

She walked along the road until it connected to another road, then took her place with others who walked the ragged countryside.